Upon a Field of Gold

A Novel Based on True Events

RICHARD NICHOLAS STRACK

BOOK PUBLISHERS NETWORK
Changing the World One Book at a Time

Book Publishers Network
P.O. Box 2256
Bothell • WA • 98041
Ph • 425-483-3040
www.bookpublishersnetwork.com

10 9 8 7 6 5 4 3 2 1
Printed in the United States of America

LCCN 2017931992
ISBN 978-1-945271-35-9

Editor: Julie Scandora
Cover Design: Laura Zugzda, Bill Nepton
Design & Layout: Melissa Vail Coffman

This book is dedicated to my wife, Stacie, my son, Richie, and my daughter, Sadie, and to the memory of my father, Nicholas, my mother, Verna, and my sisters, Nancy and Carol, and my dear friend, George Sawicki.

Let me remember the things that I don't know.
—R. N. Strack

Forward . . . and Back

I've been a card-carrying skeptic a good part of my life. My mantra has been to believe in nothing that I hear and in only half of what I see, especially because the eyes can be so deceiving. I'm full of cynicism, too. If you told me you would love me for a thousand years, I'd respond, "Oh yeah? So what happens after that?"

A few years ago, my wife held a psychic party in our home. She asked me if I wanted to have a private session with an old lady who communicates with the dead. "Oh, sign me right up," I said with sarcasm. I took up the challenge to prove the lady was a fraud.

As soon as our session began, she told me that I had lived a former life in the Civil War as a young Confederate soldier. I smirked at that remark. I've lived in the Northeast my entire life, and the only south I knew was the direction to drive on the Parkway when I traveled to the Jersey shore.

I sat back with my body language informing the old lady that if she told me the black chair I was sitting in was black, I could prove her wrong.

Suddenly, she jumped up and stood in front of me and said, "Your father is here in the room with us."

Now that's cruel, I thought. My dad died when I was a first-year college student, after we had rung up a big zero of a relationship.

The next thing the old lady said caused my hands to shake. "Your father had some kind of breathing problem," she said.

"That's why I'm standing. He couldn't sit down because he couldn't breathe, so he stood most of the time."

My dad died of emphysema, and for the last seven years of his life, he would sit only to eat a meal or to drive a car. When he was home, he would stand and lean on the backs of chairs, often with a noisy struggle to catch his next breath.

First, I wondered who had told the old psychic about his condition. Then I realized no one could have said anything to her about his standing because I never told anyone—absolutely no one who was still alive knew about his sickness.

She went on to tell me how my dad felt awful that he was never a father to me, but that he wanted to help me now.

So, with tears falling freely, Mr. Skeptic, Mr. Lady-I'm-Going-to-Prove-You're-a-Fraud asked in his little boy's voice, "How will he help me?"

"You want to write after you've finished your teaching career, don't you?" she asked.

"Yes."

"Your father wants you to know he will still be standing, but this time he will stand behind you with great pride whenever you sit down to write."

The old lady had me completely now. From that moment on, she could have told me I was going to be the first person ever to sprout wings to fly, and I would have started flapping my arms.

Several other predictions she made have all come true for me during the years since that session. I regret I have not seen her since to ask her more questions about my future and to tell her what I have learned about my past—not my past as Richard Nicholas Strack; my past as that young Confederate soldier.

So here are the stories of my two souls, fact blended together with fiction, offered to entertain you and perhaps to open your mind, to wonder whether every human life has only one beginning and only one end.

You can assume my dad feels the same way I do. Through every single word I've written in this book, he's been standing right behind me.

Winchester County, Virginia
June 15, 1863

Straight ahead, a dark figure stepped into the morning sunlight. Joshua Park butted the stock of his rifle against his shoulder. He aimed at the Yank, now shadowed in blue. Against his will, he squeezed the trigger. His shoulder slammed backward from the recoil. The sound of the exploding bullet pierced his brain. In spite of the fear of what he might see next, he opened his eyes.

About thirty yards away, the Yank let out an inhuman scream that echoed through the thicket. Blood spurted through his fingers from a bright red hole above his knee where the white of exposed bone gleamed. He staggered on his buckling leg but managed to stay upright.

In a silent plea for help, Joshua looked over at Carter.

"Well, well, now," yelled Carter through a toothless smile. "Ya missed killin' the sumbitch on purpose, didn't ya, boy?" Carter smirked at Joshua and then fired a Minié ball through the soldier's left eye, snapping the man's head back before he dropped to the ground. His body shook on the short grass for a long, awful moment before it came to a rest.

Joshua turned away and threw down his Sharps carbine. He bent over and grabbed his knees with both hands, and with one violent upward rush from deep inside his belly, he vomited all over his shoes.

Clay County, Alabama
Three Months Earlier

She came through the wheat field like a wild horse, her mane of blond hair flying everywhere. Her grand entrance presented her to Joshua as no Southern belle; that was for sure. With a splotch of jam stuck to her chin, she wore a boy's cotton shirt with overalls torn at both knees. When she stopped her run under Ol' Oakie, Joshua reckoned she was going to scream, "Fire!"

Instead, she blurted, "I'm Becky. I live across the field. Me and my ma moved in a coupla weeks ago. I seen you come here a lot, but you never seen me."

All that with just one breath, Joshua thought.

He lifted his eyebrows and asked, "Why is it that you see me, but I never see you?" Pretending to show little interest in the answer to his question, he sat back against Ol' Oakie with his hands clasped behind his head.

"I know a lot of things 'bout folks who don't know nuthin' 'bout me," she said. "I make it my business to know, but when it comes to me, it's nobody's business."

"So why are you here if you don't want nobody to know you?"

Becky cocked her head like a confused puppy. "I reckon yer someone who can get to know me." She took a step forward. "That's if you want."

"Well, if you know 'bout me, then tell me what you know."

Becky twisted a strand of her hair around her finger. "I know you come through that there field every day to this big tree to sit under and look out over the field. I can tell yer a thinker, and even a dreamer, kinda like me."

Joshua stretched out his legs. He liked girly girls, but this one might want to go fishing with him or help him set traps down by the river.

"What's with the boy's clothes? You got yer brother's hand-me-downs?"

"Nope. Only child, and there ain't no brothers or sisters comin'. My pa died when I was little when he got throwed from a horse and hit his head on a rock. Far as clothes go, my ma knows she ain't gettin' me in none o' them frilly dresses, especially on days when I go explorin' for some new frogs to add to my collection."

"You know," he said, "I just don't let anyone come under my tree. It's kinda private here, where I do my thinkin' and wonderin'." He looked out to the field. "I got me some grand plans for myself, and Ol' Oakie here helps me think 'em through."

"I like that," said Becky.

"You like that I got grand plans?"

"Ol' Oakie. I like the name." Becky ran her fingers along the tree's massive trunk. "Mind if I get a bird's eye look at this here field?"

Before Joshua could answer, Becky scooted up the tree like a raccoon escaping a shotgun. She didn't stop at the first limb. Up she went until he could make out only the bottoms of her shoes between the top branches.

"Come on up!" she hollered. "That's if you can make it this far."

Before another leaf from Ol' Oakie could fall to the ground, Joshua slid his backside onto the limb next to Becky.

They stayed there until the sun dropped under the horizon, yakking about everything from the best-tasting blackberry pies to their favorite clouds, to what it might be like to live on the moon. They ended with a talk about spirits and souls.

"I don't reckon when yer dead yer dead," said Joshua. "Just look across this field. Spirits move with the wind. They're folks who lived and died here a hundred year or so ago, or maybe someone who was just passin' through and sorta liked this place and come back after he died. They're out there. You can feel 'em driftin' across the field every time there's a new wind."

"I like it here," said Becky. "I kinda hope when my spirit lives after me, it comes right back to this place."

Every day thereafter, Becky came by Ol' Oakie in the afternoons. Joshua tried to resist the thought, but he knew he was getting sweet on her, and he could tell she had a hankering for him, too.

He didn't care what they did together, and neither did she. Sometimes on lazy days, they would drop a line at the catfish hole, not paying any special attention to whether they got a bite. One afternoon, a big ol' whiskerface must've grabbed Joshua's cornball, taking the hook, line, and cane pole down the river without his noticing.

While this was happening, they were locked in their first kiss. Becky's eyes were both shut, and one of Joshua's was squeezed shut, too, but the other one, wide open, saw the pole being dragged downstream. When he tried to pull away, Becky wouldn't let go.

After he finally broke free, he ran down the riverbank and skipped into the murky water. The pole floated by where he could reach it if he took one more step. He did. His foot sank into a hole, and his body collapsed until he was chin deep in the river.

He heard Becky laughing. As the water gushed into his britches, Joshua slapped his arms against the green surface of the downstream current. "Help! Help me, Becky!" Down he sank until the water spilled over the top of his head.

"Parky, stop foolin' around!" she shouted. "Stop yer foolin' now, Parky!" she shouted again.

He saw her distorted figure through the water against the blue sky.

She rushed to the riverbank with her hands outstretched. Joshua expelled a breath, blowing a large bubble to the surface. He looked through the water again. Becky was waving her arms. With one hard push off the bottom, Joshua surfaced. He grabbed

Becky's arm, yanking her into the river. The water muffled her scream as it rushed over her head.

Joshua fell onto his back and spit out a loud laugh. Becky surfaced and swung her fist at his head but missed. The current pushed her into his arms. They trudged onto the bank with Joshua dragging a flapping catfish behind him.

"There's somethin' we still gotta finish," he said, dropping the fish down the bank where it wriggled back into the water. He pulled her soaking wet body toward him, just so their lips could barely touch. Becky swung her arms around his neck.

When he thought it to be proper, Joshua opened his eyes. The sun had dropped below the horizon, leaving them under an umbrella of soft evening light.

Three days later, as he sat with Becky on his back porch, she hollered, "Let's go!"

She took off toward Ol' Oakie, running as fast as a deer. She scampered up the tree, clawing her hands and feet as if she had a cat's paws.

Joshua sped after and stopped to catch his breath below Ol' Oakie's massive arms.

"You comin' up, Parky, or do I have to come down?" She giggled in that high, flirty voice he'd come to like so much.

"You come down," he yelled back.

She flipped up her backside and leaped to the ground. He stepped over to catch her, but she slipped right out of his arms and landed on a bed of moss. "You okay?" he asked, concerned. Becky made a face at him and let out a groan between her teeth. As he bent down to help her up, she jumped from the ground and pushed him down, glaring at him with her perfect blue eyes. She turned and ran off into the field with Joshua following in half-hearted pursuit. He lost sight of her in the tall grain. When he stopped to catch a breath, he heard her scream.

With his heart in his throat, Joshua ran toward her second and third screams. He found Becky crawled up in a ball under a swarm of hovering hornets. A few of them turned in midair and attacked him. He snatched one with his right hand, squashing it into his fist. One hornet after another, he swiped off Becky and himself. Bug guts oozed through his fingers into a thick, sticky mess until the last few hornets buzzed off into the air.

The fear from Becky's face seemed to fly away with their wings.

"Can you catch me a hummingbird with them hands of yers?" she asked, oblivious to the welts rising on her arms and legs.

"Dunno if I could," said Joshua, helping her to her feet. "I might."

"How about a spirit, flyin' low?"

"I reckon you couldn't catch a spirit with yer hands, girl," he said, grinning.

"Well, from what I just seen, I think you might—and if you did, we could sit that ol' spirit down and have him tell us his story about how he come to this field."

Becky took his hand, and they walked back to Ol' Oakie. The air had stilled over the field; the reeds stood straight to the sky. No birds or butterflies fluttered over their heads. Even the crickets and locusts were quiet.

"Feel the peace, Parky?" She pulled Joshua down by her side, into a bed of Ol' Oakie's exposed roots. "This is the perfect moment to open our souls to the spirits," she whispered and rested her head on his shoulder. "You ever wonder if yer spirit's gonna come here after you die?" she asked in a low voice.

He looked up to see a willowy cloud floating directly above them. "I sure hope it does, and if yers comes too, I'm gonna pick you up in a big white cloud like that one, and together we can drift right over this field forever and ever."

They lay and listened to the silence until a sudden wind charged across the field, swirling through Ol' Oakie's branches. Fresh air fell upon them like a dry rain, cooling their faces from the scorching sun. Joshua looked over at Becky, at her yellow hair lifted by puffs of air. He thought she was the prettiest damn thing he'd ever seen.

The field moved in rhythm with the wind.

"Listen," whispered Joshua.

"Look," said Becky.

Spirits danced before them to the delight of the afternoon heavens, and it was then that Joshua realized the power of his immortality.

The next day, Ma busied herself with organizing plans for the day with her colored folk, Joseph Charles and Sophie, but she made sure she found time for Joshua.

After his bath, Sophie came in to clean up, and sent him to his ma to hear a story about the chickens in the coop out back.

"Ever' time Joseph Charles goes out to get one for supper, this one hen jumps out front," Ma said to Joshua. "It's like she's sayin', 'Take me, take me!' Joseph Charles jus' pushes her aside and grabs another cuz he says the hen's not fat enough yet." Ma went on to say she was skeptical so much that she decided to go with Joseph Charles and see for herself. "Here comes that hen again, right out to the front," she reported, "So I tell Joseph Charles to let that hen live. If she's gonna stand up for her peeps like that, then she deserves to live to a right honorable old age.

"That day, I told Joseph Charles the same thing I'm gonna tell you, son. If you believe in what you think is right, then never let anyone convince you to back down from that belief. There's an old sayin' I want you to remember—those that bleed red, sleep sound in their bed. Those that bleed black have no spine in their back."

Joshua didn't get the "black" part, but he understood the gist of what Ma was saying about the other color. A red-blooded person is strong in the mind and won't back down from anything or from anybody. She went on to say that she'd needed that same kind of faith and courage when she gave birth to him. It was like pushing out a wild pig, she said, though he didn't care for the comparison. After he had squeezed through her, he squealed so loud she had to take a look to see if he had but two legs and not four.

"And when you were just seven years old, I knew you were no simple mind, neither. You had these wild thoughts going on inside that head of yers. You'd look up to the sky and point to a particular cloud and say, 'I'm gonna get on that cloud, and it's gonna ride me around the sun and back.' Then there were another time I heard you talkin' to that big ol' tree out back, and you seemed to be actin' like it were talkin' back to you. 'My, my,' I said to myself, 'my son's either downright crazy, or the good Lord made him out to be somebody special, not like most folks who just eat and sleep and try to survive another day before death comes a-callin.'"

Ma always took close notice of what he was doing, but when it came to his pa, Joshua sometimes thought his father needed to be reminded that he *had* a son. Pa never seemed to be home much, but when he was, it was one order after another for Joshua. Do your schooling. Do you your chores. He appeared troubled by a lot of things, especially the war. He said as soon as Jeff Davis come a-calling, Joshua would have to go help win the Cause.

The Cause confused Joshua until Joseph Charles sat him down to explain it.

First, the old black man rubbed his gray beard with his thumb and pointer finger. That's how Joshua knew Joseph Charles was thinking deep thoughts. Then he said in his careful way, "Your pa is worried that if the people up North come down here to impose their will, we're gonna have to give up life as we know it and follow whatever laws Mr. Lincoln orders."

That was the best reason Joshua had heard yet as to why they had to kill Yankees. He figured that was all there was to tell. But when he got up to leave, Joseph Charles put him back down in the seat. "There's more to say," he said in a whisper. He motioned for Joshua to move his head closer. "Many people of the dark skin are being mistreated and kept away from their families to serve the plantation owners."

"I don't see you mistreated." Joshua said.

"Your ma and pa treat me rightly, but I'm a man of privilege in that respect. Those workin' the fields, they have nuthin' but broken backs and shacks to live in that are so small you can't turn around without bumpin' into somethin'. Sometimes I feel, you know, guilty a bit, to be takin' care of this household while others like me work in the hot fields and live in fear of the whip."

"Pa said the Negro is a lesser human being than us white folks."

Joseph Charles appeared to be disturbed by that statement.

"I don't reckon yer any less than me," Joshua said. "To be truthful, I don't get it. Once I thought Negroes were born like horses to do the hard work in the fields cuz that's what I been told, but now I wonder why Pa and Uncle Jim don't help out with the work. I'd help, too, but Pa won't let me. It'd seem like the right thing to do to make it easier for everyone."

Joseph Charles patted Joshua on the head. "Yer a kind boy."

"So what would you do if you weren't here?" Joshua asked.

"Don't rightly know, son," he said. After Joshua could see him thinking a bit more, Joseph Charles went on. "My people want to be happy. They want to be free like your people. But what frightens me is what would we do if we had the will to do what we want and go where we want? Most of us ain't prepared for that. If the Confederacy loses this war, we're gonna be like chickens runnin' around with our heads cut off. Then again, we let the good Lord take care of our kind, and we pray for our freedom every day. We never lose faith."

He pinched Joshua's cheek. "I say the same to you, son. Never lose faith in what you believe in."

Joshua had to admit he liked Joseph Charles more than he liked his pa. Just looking into the black man's bright green eyes picked up his spirits. It was as if Joshua could see into the man's soul, one that was as kind as any he had ever known.

⌗

The news came the next evening from Uncle Jim. He brought everyone together in the parlor, white and colored folks alike, and told them solemnly, "The Yanks blew up the bridge to

Tuscaloosa yesterday." Tears began rolling down his weathered cheeks as he put his hand on Joshua's shoulder. "Yer ma and pa were on the train when the bridge collapsed, son. They were both killed."

Wails filled the room. Sophie passed out and was immediately attended to by Joseph Charles.

Joshua sat in silence. He didn't feel too sad about Pa, but when he let himself think that he'd never see his ma again, he dropped his face into his hands and squeezed back his tears.

<hr />

When Joshua awoke the next morning, he could hear a voice inside his head telling him that everything about his life as he knew it was about to change.

Hands in his pockets, he ambled through the misty morning field until he found himself under his tree. Ol' Oakie had never seemed sad until this day. Its leaves curled downward in their disappointment with the deep gray sky.

Joshua had come early. He wanted to be here without Becky for a while, to be alone with his thoughts.

Drops of water fell upon his shoulders. He looked up through the limbs and branches. The heavy mist dripped onto his face from Ol' Oakie's sad leaves. He closed his eyes as the drops of water fell unwelcomed, stinging his skin, and yet he accepted the offering, thinking his tree was shedding its tears for what he was about to do this day.

Joshua had come to say goodbye.

"I reckoned you'd be here early today," said a voice. For just a second, he thought Ol' Oakie had spoken to him.

Joshua blinked the water from his eyes to find Becky standing before him, wet from the mist that was now turning to rain. She looked as dark as the clouds behind her. A gust of wind whistled across the field, making her shiver.

"You know, it's really stupid to think like we do, like this is a place where time don't matter and life goes on forever," he said.

"Parky, yer wrong. This place is a circle of heaven in the middle of this hellish world, with all its hatred and its . . . its horrible game, where killing each other's supposed to win somethin' for some greedy old men who push their powers into the faces of scared, innocent boys who go out to kill their own kind—and for what, to wave a vict'ry flag?"

He marveled again at her ability to say so much with a single breath.

"This country," she went on, "fought for a chance to grow into somethin' special, to be on our own with our people free to live like we want. Now we're back where we used to be, only this time it's our own folk demandin' how we should live. Boys have to kill boys just 'cuz somebody draws a line in the sand." Becky wiped her mouth with the back of her hand. She stood in protest against the hard rain now falling between Ol' Oakie's heavy limbs.

Lightning blistered the horizon. Thunder rumbled across the field.

"I'm gonna pray, Parky, that this country finds its common sense before all of us who wait for our boys to come home got nobody left to wait for."

Joshua turned and sprang up the tree. He climbed high onto his favorite limb and then looked down for Becky. She was gone.

Ol' Oakie groaned against the fierce wind, its branches slapping their leaves against his bare arms and legs. "Becky! Becky! Where are you?" he screamed through the snarling wind. Ol' Oakie groaned again against the fury of the storm. The rain pelted the field. Another flash and rumble ripped across the blackened sky.

"You don't have to go," said Becky, who appeared next to him as if she had flown up the tree on wings.

Maybe she had, he thought. "I don't have a choice," he said.

"What can they do to you?"

"Refusal to serve is the same as desertion. Prison or execution."

"What about us?"

"There will be no *us* if we lose the war."

"Don't matter to me who wins or loses. There can always be us, Parky."

Claps of thunder bellowed again over the field. As Becky leaned into Joshua, he flipped up his arm and shuffled down the tree, jumping the last ten feet to the ground. He ran through the field as fast as he could, knowing she would be close behind. He ran and ran until he came to the back porch of his house.

Becky jumped up alongside. Soaked to the bone from the now relenting rain, they bent over to catch their breaths.

"There *is* no us after tomorrow, can't you see?" Joshua's voice screeched through the distant thunder. "We can't live under a stupid tree for the rest of our lives!" He wiped the rain from his face with the back of his hand. "It was just a dream, Becky. Ever'thing we did together, ever'thing we talked about. Nuthin' but a dream."

She leaned back against the railing. The rain had pasted her hair onto both sides of her face. The sun shafted through the vanishing clouds, casting a soft glow of light around the figure of her body.

Still pretty as an angel, he thought.

"We will always be dreamers, Joshua Park." She took a step toward him. "Dreamers never die. I'll wait 'til you come back."

"What if I don't come back?"

"You *will* come back—sometime, somewhere. If it takes forever, you'll find me, and I'll be waiting for you."

A strange energy moved inside his body.

He pulled his wet shirt over his head. Becky unbuttoned her cotton blouse down to her waist. Off came everything until they stood naked under an emerging blue sky. Acting on nothing more than instinct, Joshua lifted Becky against the railing of the porch. She closed her eyes. His innocence held him back from where he had never gone before, but she reached behind him and pulled them together.

Fevered by the heat from her body, he moved with the rhythm of her heartbeat. Then, driven by a never-before known force, he released everything he had left inside him into his faith that they would someday be together again.

The very next day, Joshua was to report to the Alabama Thirteenth for training. He thought Pa's spirit must have had something to do with the order coming that quickly.

Becky stood at attention on his back porch. Joshua had never seen her so pretty and so girly. Her hair was curled at the ends. A bright yellow flower tucked above her right ear reflected upon the cheeks of her face. She wore a blue dress with ruffles upon her shoulders. Clutched tightly in her left hand was a piece of folded paper.

"Whatcha got?" he asked.

"Just a letter."

He reached out his hand to take it, but she pulled back. "You gotta promise not to read it 'til you get to yer camp."

"I promise."

She handed him the paper.

They stood there staring at each other as if there was no more to say.

Then Becky stepped forward and kissed him right on his lips. "I love you, Parky," she said quietly. She took a step back. "You take care of yerself, you hear?" She turned to leave, but she stopped herself and looked back.

"And don't ever die on me!"

"Becky, wait."

She turned around to face him, and he put his arms around her. Joshua kissed her so hard he could feel her gasp for a breath. He took her left hand and stuffed it with his own piece of paper. "That's my letter to you," he said. "And you promise not to read it unless you don't hear from me again."

Becky wiped a tear from her eye. "I promise, Parky."

Then, with a burst of wind behind her, Becky fled through the field, just as she had when she had arrived on their first day. All that remained were the tall reeds swaying back and forth until they finally came to rest, erasing the path made by her fleeting footsteps.

Gettysburg, Pennsylvania
July 3, 1863 – 1:30 p.m.

Joshua could no longer see to where the line ended. He guessed most of the boys were back in the trees. To the right stood his regiment, the Alabama Thirteenth, in straight order, military rank and file, arms ready at their shoulders, waiting for the command to march.

The summer sun burned through a patch of stubborn clouds. Shrouds of light shimmered off three straight miles of rifle bayonets. Joshua liked to think this was the Almighty's approval of their charge to a glorious victory.

Cal Jenkins glanced over at him. With one simple smile, this man could convince every boy in the regiment that he was invincible. He stroked his moustache and stared at the peak of the hill. There it was, that famous Jenkins smile. Joshua waited for a truth that always came next.

"Boy, I'll see you on the other side," Jenkins said to Joshua before he spat on the ground.

He was the best, Jenkins was. When Joshua had the Virginia quickstep running out of his backside for three straight days, Jenkins brought him fresh water to drink. When Joshua felt better, Jenkins passed him his hardtack saying, "Ya gotta eat to stay strong, boy." Then there was the night he dragged Joshua into a tent after he found the exhausted boy asleep outside under a windswept downpour. Jenkins stripped him down and wrapped him in a dry blanket.

Jenkins would fight the enemy with the relentlessness of a rabid boar, but under his impenetrable badge of courage lay a heart as soft as cotton. Whenever he spoke, he sounded as if he were speaking words from a book.

"Men were born to love and live, not to hate and die," he said at camp last night. All ears and eyes opened whenever Jenkins delivered his life lesson for the day. "Just think. We gotta kill so we can live in peace. Makes no sense to me. Men with differences of opinion need to come to an understanding without guns gettin' between 'em.

"Shoot, when I was a boy," he went on, "there were this fella name a Ernie Smalls who lived down the road. Well, he pointed his rifle at me one day, tellin' me I were a dead one if I come near his sister again. I told him to put down the gun and we'd settle this like two men should. We punched at each other for what seemed like the whole mornin' before we both fell down tired as two old dogs." Jenkins shot out another of those smiles. "We shook hands, and it was done. And that sister of his is now my Sally, my bride of four years tomorrow."

After the briefing at sunrise, Jenkins pulled Joshua aside. "We gotta git you back safe to yer Miss Becky. If it's meant for you to be together, then trust in the Lord's will in this here fight for it to be done."

"Oh, it's meant to be," said Joshua. "We got promises from the spirits in the field behind Ol' Oakie."

"Well, it damn well better be," chirped Carter, "cuz I git up ever' mornin' with her name stuck in my head from you yakkin' about her all night long in yer dreams."

Joshua pondered the long climb up the field to the hill that Turner called "the road of final reckoning," what Waterson named "the mount of eternal salvation" and Carter spat out as "the path through the devil's asshole."

Joshua tried not to think about the boys who wouldn't see the sun rise tomorrow and, God forbid, how he might be one of them.

The very idea of dying on foreign ground brought these soldiers of different beliefs together with a single purpose. Joshua figured that war forged friendships simply because of the fear of isolation, especially since the thought of dying stuck like molasses in their minds. Just as in most families, the boys bickered with each other and sometimes butted their heads, but from a code of understood loyalty sealed with blood spilt on the battlefield, they were brothers brought together to beat down the devil's bitch. And only one thing drove them to kill.

Get back home.

Every squeeze of the trigger brought Joshua a step closer to Becky, to Ol' Oakie, and to their field of dreams.

No one said it, but everyone knew it. This day, this hill, would end it all. When Joshua got back home, the first thing he was going to do was open the door and tell Joseph Charles to go find his own family.

In the distance, at what seemed like a cannonball's shot to the moon, snaps of gunfire sent puffs of smoke into the muggy air. The Yanks were answering the Rebel artillery that had blasted the hill since sunrise.

While reading his Bible at breakfast, Waterson remarked, "This fight's gonna be nothin' to cause a widow to wave goodbye to her dead soldier."

Words said by a man whose heart, Joshua believed, beat with the hand of God upon it.

July 3 – 2 p.m.

They still stood, but no longer did they stand still. Some of the boys began to fidget. Joshua looked down at his toes. He moved them through holes in what were left of his shoes. Thirty miles a day, all the way from Virginia, he'd walked in those shoes. What a good fortune he and some of the boys enjoyed by having soles under their feet.

Except for Carter, of course. He couldn't wait until he could shove one of his filthy feet, yellow toenails and all, through the jaws of a bluebelly he would shoot dead.

All gunfire ceased, leaving a strange silence across the field. The welcomed calm gave Joshua another moment to turn his thoughts to Becky. How refreshing her face would be to his tired eyes when he got back home. He swore he could smell her hair through a fresh breeze that had just swept across his face.

A Yankee cannon blast landed forty yards from their line. Startled, the boys jumped back, but not Carter. "Woohoo!" the crazy man shouted. He stepped to the edge of the field and cursed the billows of gray smoke that waffled into the sky. The burning odor found its way to their noses. Carter took a deep breath and cupped his hands around his mouth. "Bring it on, ya Yankee bastards! Woo-hoo!"

Joshua's knees started to shake like a bowl of Aunt Sara's jam. He swallowed hard, and the lump in his throat sank like a rock to the bottom of his belly. He had to tell himself again and again that he was no greenie, no sir. He'd amazed the boys in the regiment with his hand-and-eye skill. He'd grabbed a single mosquito diving at Turner's face. He'd knocked an apple off a tree with a small stone at twenty yards. His musket had dropped at least one

Yank. Besides the one he hit in the knee who Carter finished off, he'd shot right through the barrel of a rifle held by a bluebelly, and another time his musket blew off a Yankee officer's hat just before Turner finished him with a bullet through the neck.

Carter told the general that Joshua would be the best shot to take out a sniper under cover. When he was approached about it, Joshua shook his head. He'd sooner take on another round of the quickstep than kill a man who never knew the bullet was coming.

Joshua coughed up another lump from his throat. Jenkins grabbed his shoulder and shook him so hard he thought he might fall on top of his own bayonet. "You know what I always tell you 'bout how war can change a man," Jenkins said. "You and me don't like killin', boy. Let's keep it that way. When this shit's over with, we wanna still have warm blood runnin' through our veins, not like that cold-blooded bastard Carter. If he had it his way, this damn war would go on forever."

Joshua felt good from that remark and, for that matter, from any remark that came from his friend. Yesterday morning, he had asked Jenkins to be his best man at the wedding. Becky would certainly approve. Jenkins had laughed. "Well, boy, I guess I will have to consent to yer request 'cause I ain't never been a best man for nuthin' else I ever done. Second-best, maybe, worst sometimes, but never best."

From the left flank, General Pickett galloped in front of the line on his gray horse, waving his saber in circles above his head. Joshua thought the general looked majestic, from the gleam of his silvery sword blade right down to the sheen of his black boots. The boys wanted to let out a roar that General Lee could hear from his headquarters a half a mile away, but the order had come down to remain silent. They opened their ears to the general.

"Men of the Mississippi, of the Alabama, of the Kentucky, of the Georgia, of the Carolina, of the Virginia regiments! Remain at ease until given the order to advance, my brave gentlemen!"

No one had ever called Joshua a gentleman before. In this instance, he adored General Pickett for more than just the officer's reputation. Joshua peered up the hill. He spit up another lump. This one landed on his shoe. He wiped it off on the side of his pants leg, hoping no one saw.

The afternoon sun blazed into the shade of the woods right after Colonel Fry announced another delay of the advance. The boys passed the word along the line, and Joshua breathed easier. He was in no hurry to depart the cool shade beneath the trees.

The field lay under a heavy blanket of air, so thick that Carter said he wanted to strip down naked and smother the bluebellies with the dripping sweat from his armpits. The man was fearless. Jenkins once told the boys that Carter had laughed in his own daddy's face when the ol' man got to smacking his son's backside with a hickory stick. Turner told a story around the campfire about the day Carter killed two Yanks at once after he grabbed them both by their collars. He cracked their heads together so hard he broke their necks. Their heads dropped down the same way you'd see a chicken give way after Joseph Charles twisted the poor bird's neck before he stripped it for supper.

Carter told Joshua that when the war was over, he'd get himself a cute little belle from Bammy, and the two of them would blow out about nine little ones, or at least enough to make sure he had several boys. Just in case another war broke out, he wanted to have enough of his kin to fight it.

Earlier this morning, he'd roused Joshua and the boys to announce the field would bleed blue and red this afternoon. When the boys reached the top of the hill, he was going to let out such a Rebel yell that Lincoln himself would skedaddle out of Washington like a wild pig with Minié balls smoking out of his backside.

When the boys made fun of each other to break the boredom, Joshua was often on the receiving end. On the night before

General Lee led the troops across the Pennsylvania border, Carter pulled Joshua aside, but he made sure they stood in front of some of the boys because he loved to speak before an audience. "We got to git some flesh on them scrawny bones of yers, boy, cuz someday soon yer gonna strip down and show yer Miss Becky what it takes to please a Southern lady. I reckon she gonna give you all that back and then some," he blabbered, "if what you described to me about that spunk locked up inside that body o' hers is true." Carter spit to the side. "Ya want some advice from me, take yer little lady on down to the river. Ya git nekkid. Ya do the deed and then jump right in the river after."

The boys laughed on cue.

"Ya see, Park? You wash off the jeebies from yer privates, and ya git yer bath for the month done, too."

The rest of the boys had gathered around by then, except for Waterson. He read his Bible on the other side of the campfire. Waterson was the regiment's self-proclaimed minister. This war, he said, was not a fight between good and evil; he was quick to point out that bluebellies were children of God too, and if they needed to be killed, then they were to be killed with respect and their bodies to be prayed over because, as he said, "We are all brothers in the eyes of our Maker."

When he was through advising Joshua, Carter slugged down some coffee. He pointed to Waterson. "Looky there. He's talkin' to God again."

Waterson lifted his head up from the book. "Just sayin' some prayers for you and yer Yankee brothers, Carter."

"Them Yankee bastards ain't my brothers!" hollered Carter. "Them's the devil what's come to take what's rightfully ours!"

"They are flesh and blood just like you and me," answered Waterson. "They got families, wives, children, just like us. They're bein' told to kill, just like us. They bleed red, just like us."

Carter walked around the fire. He jabbed his finger into Waterson's shoulder. "Shit," said Carter, spitting into the campfire. "It's been predicted in that there book of yers the devil will come to the Earth and bring hunnerts a years of evil and terror unless he be stopped."

"Carter, my friend, the Lord don't hold for killin' no human bein' who were given birth just like you and me. When this war is done, he's gonna be cryin' for ever'one that lost loved ones to the bullet. So we gotta keep our boys from dyin', 'specially the young ones like Park over there. He gotta get back to his angel Rebecca."

Joshua wondered if Waterson had let out some kind of intuition he got from his Good Book by calling Becky an angel. She did kind of fly into his life that spring day.

"I never looked at her, and she never looked at me the whole time we sat on Ol' Oakie," Joshua had told Jenkins about his first afternoon with her. "We were just talkin' and kickin' back our legs."

"Well, look here, boy," Jenkins had said. "Now, I ain't never gonna get asked what yer supposed to think when it comes to what you might call a man and a woman thing," he said. "But from what I hear 'bout you and Miss Becky, it don't matter if yer lookin' in her eyes or she's lookin' in yers." He had smiled one of those grins that meant another truth was coming out of his mouth next. "You two look at one 'nuther from inside yer minds. Even right now, standin' before this field, you see her, and she sees you." Jenkins pointed to the hill. "It almost makes ya think if she were there now, ya could walk right up to meet her, and the bluebellies wouldn't bother ya at all."

∞

Colonel Fry stood before the line again. "Men, what happens today on this field will forever mark a place for you in history. You will fight for your freedom, for your state, for the Confederacy, for President Davis!"

No longer ordered to stay quiet, the troops let out a Rebel yell that sent chills so far down Joshua's spine his toes twitched.

The colonel raised his hands to restore order. "For your wives, for your babies, for your honeys, and for your legacies. For you who spill your blood on this field today, you will make your mark of courage upon our greatest victory. For you who perish under the sun of God's heavenly glory, your deaths will not be forgotten, and your lives will become eternal through your sacrifice."

The colonel paused to scan the line.

"May God protect you from the wrath of the enemy! May he empower you with his almighty strength! May he walk by your side as you ascend to the top of that hill to stand in victory right beside our honored flag of the Confederacy!"

The line cheered again. The colonel about-faced. The flag-man stepped forward, holding the blue and white cross with stars that would be their beacon of light, their point of direction. Joshua thought what an honor it was for this boy. If, God forbid, he should fall, the next in line would retrieve the flag and carry it forward.

With rifle at parade rest, Joshua stood at attention, awaiting the command to march.

A cannon shell soared through the air and exploded some sixty yards ahead of the line. Joshua squeezed his eyes shut. The ringing in his ears dulled all sound around him. He shook his head, trying to it chase the noise away. He barely could hear a shout come from down the line, probably Carter swearing at those damn Yankees again.

Another shell sailed far off to the right.

He could make out a road ahead that cut through the field. What looked like a long, split-rail wooden fence was running down a path as far as he could see. What a sight it would be when the Yanks saw twelve thousand Rebel boys climbing over that fence. That scene alone ought to scare them enough to make them fall back from the hill and retreat.

Yesterday, a skirmish had broken out on the big rock about a mile from the field. The regiment took some serious losses from the engagement, and when the North Carolina returned with bodies, Joshua took a hard look at the remains. There was one particular dead boy, about Joshua's age, he remembered from camp. *He put his feet inside his britches just like me this mornin',* Joshua thought, *but the poor boy didn't know it would be the last day he would ever pull 'em up.*

Joshua stared down at the body. The thing about death was when you stared at it, it stared at you back. A dead body can say things, too. First, Joshua studied the boy's eyes, wide open, looking up at the sky as if to say, "Lord, I'm a-comin' now." His hands were clenched tightly, most likely squeezing that last bit of pain out of his body. His mouth, with dried blood on his bitten lip, looked to be still trying to suck in a breath of life that was coming no more. A bit of bullet stuck out from underneath his jaw, marked by a reddish brown blister. When the bullet had hit, blood must have spurted from his throat like water gushing from a spring.

The last thing this dead boy tasted must have been his own blood clogging his throat like mud, choking him until he coughed it up leaving a red stain on his shirt just above his chest.

Joshua wondered if anyone dying knew he was dying. In war, a soldier only gets a blink of an eye's moment to let his brain think that thought. It must be pain, fear, and then peace in that order, all in a quick minute. And if time allows, what would be the final thought that burns out the fire in his brain? A desperate wish, like, "Please, God, have mercy on my soul," an angry shout against fate, or a final declaration to someone like, "I love you. I will always love you 'til the end of time"?

Then what? The spirit leaves the body, drifting along with the wind until finding a peaceful place to forever rest.

There should be a special place in heaven just for dead soldiers, he decided, a beautiful field with some big ol' trees like Ol' Oakie providing plenty of shade with cool breezes to soothe away any fears left in their souls. Those who lay down their lives for a cause have given the greatest sacrifice they can give. The married ones widow their wives and make fatherless their children while those who have yet to start their own families will never get the chance.

A dead soldier should not just depart this world as a memory, but he should leave behind some permanent reminder of a life that was so terribly shortened by war.

Joshua thought that no one's life, not even a Yank's, should end without meaning. When the last shovel of dirt falls upon his grave and his body becomes food for the worms, his ascended soul should see what natural beauty he leaves behind. That's sort of eternal life, just in a different way.

Jenkins, in his way, had explained immortality just yesterday.

"Why else would any self-respectin' fool march into an open field to face the bullet?"

July 3 – 3 p.m.

What began as a hazy morning sky, disturbed only by small flocks of blackbirds scooting across the field, turned into an afternoon storm of smoky explosions from Rebel cannon fire, so loud that Joshua slapped his ears to try to stop them from ringing again.

After two days of tactical advantage, the generals had planned a grand final attack. Drive the Yanks back with artillery. Finish them off with an army a mile wide. Capture the hill. March on and take Washington.

Over the past two days, Joshua had been fortunate to avoid any major fighting. His regiment had encountered skirmishers yesterday and the day before at the big rocks. Casualties were severe, but the only dead man he knew was Samuel Tower. Tower took a Minié ball above the right ear, and when they dragged him back, he was still breathing. It was sad to see. Joshua figured that the man knew he was dying and didn't want to die alone.

Tower, with his perfect name, was a big strong man. He was often called upon to move cannons into battle lines. The other day, when a soldier from the division got sick on the march up from Virginia, Tower took up his supplies. When the same man collapsed from fatigue, Tower threw him over his shoulder like a sack of corn and carried him along until camp was set up for the night.

Now here this big man lay on the ground with that look of death in his eyes, gasping for air. At first, the wound didn't appear to be that serious until Joshua took a closer look. A piece was missing from the side of his head. Yellowish stuff had oozed out that must have been some of his brain.

Nobody knows the proper thing to say to a dying man, except some words of comfort. Henry Burton knelt down next to Tower, who lifted his hand up for Henry to take. "It's gonna be all good, Samuel," said Burton, with no sense of conviction.

Tower looked up at Burton. He opened his mouth as if to say something, but only a bubble of blood popped open from between his lips. He raised his other hand, and Burton took hold of that one too. "Samuel," said Burton. "No more pain. No more fear. Rest yer mind, and place yer soul into the hands of the Lord. He's gonna take you home."

Joshua swore he saw Tower force a smile through the blood that had run down his chin. Then he made a gurgling noise and rolled his eyes back until his big chest took one last, deep breath. Burton held onto the big man's hands for another moment before he let them go. Then Burton raised himself up to wipe his wet eyes. A circle of soldiers gathered around Tower and lowered their heads. Soon thereafter, an officer came by.

"Atten-hut!"

The boys snapped to proper attention. The officer stood at Tower's feet. "With the promise of our Confederate States of America and for the glory of God in heaven, may he bless you and deliver his peace upon your eternal soul."

Everyone saluted. Joshua reckoned that Tower was fortunate to have a formal send-off, unlike so many others, who lay dead near the Yankee lines or whose bodies were blown into bits by cannon fire. Yesterday about dusk, several bodies that had been lying in the woods to the right were dragged in from a skirmish of two days ago. Their bellies were all blown up like pregnant women ready to give birth. The stink had saturated the air so much many of the boys passed on supper that night.

Carter had told Joshua to take a good long look at the dead. "Don't you never forget their faces, boy. Let 'em sit down hard in the center of yer head. Ev'ry time you load that there rifle of yers and point it at a damn bluebelly, you pull that trigger. You pull that trigger for these men who cain't talk no more, cain't laugh no more, cain't love no more. You and me and all the rest of us here pull our triggers cuz we owe it to these men to finish off the devil's bastards." Carter narrowed his eyes. "Otherwise," he pronounced, "their dyin' don't mean shit."

$$\sim\!\!\!\!\sim$$

With his eyes fixed upon the point of destination at the hill, Joshua listened to a new silence that fell over the field. Except for the crunching of dry brush from the restless feet of his anxious regiment, the moment of peace offered him another chance to distract his mind from what lay ahead.

Becky would be proud of him. She'd be frightened for him, too.

He remembered the time he fell off Jingles when the pony reared up from being spooked by a copperhead in the tall grass. Joshua fell back and bounced right off the pony's backside to the hard ground.

Becky, riding Rainbow behind him, let out a scream that would've chased all the snakes in Clay County back under their rocks. "Parky, oh my Lord!"

Joshua reckoned she had jumped off Rainbow without even stopping the horse. Before he could calm the buzzing bees from inside his head, she appeared right there kneeling next to him. "Parky?"

Through the haze that clouded his eyes, he had seen the sun reflect off the back of her blond hair. A circle of light had formed that looked like an angel's halo around her head. For a second, he wondered if he'd died and gone to heaven and she had come along for the welcome party. The burning pain in his backside reminded him he was still alive. It hurt something awful, but he reckoned this was no time to act like a child in front of Becky. "I'm fine," he lied.

She took hold of his arm and yanked him to his feet, sending jolts of pain down both his legs.

"Let's ride to my house," she said, as if his near-death fall had never happened.

They rode on. Joshua's backside had a purple bruise on it for a week. He didn't care.

Now, he tried not to care about his parched throat or the heat of the day that boiled his guts so bad he could hear them gurgling through the restart of the distant cannon fire.

The boys began to fuss. Once more, they were getting ready to reform the line.

"'Bout time," said Jenkins. "Only got four more hours of daylight. Let's get to that damn hill so I can do some sweet dreamin' tonight of goin' back home where I'm gonna pick up my Sally and carry her to the loft and make hay with her for two days straight!"

Any of the boys close enough to hear Jenkins roared with laughter.

With rifles again placed at shoulder rest, Joshua refocused on the task at hand. He wanted to do his part to help Jenkins get back to his Sally.

July 3 – 3:30 p.m.

With the command finally given, the Alabama Thirteenth marched up the field. With regiments from all the states of the Confederacy in attendance, Joshua believed the Yanks wouldn't know what hit them when the boys got to the top of that hill. Carter kidded that after today's decisive victory, General Lee would rename Pennsylvania North Virginia after his glorious army.

Random rifle fire from the hill disturbed the calm. The artillery of the Army of Northern Virginia ceased the attack. The few Yanks who were left on that hill were about to face thousands and thousands of soldiers under the command of General Pickett.

Battle strategy didn't always make sense to Joshua. Here they were, in a wide-open field with no ground cover whatsoever, walking right into open fire. He understood the numbers thing. His schooling taught him that more numbers of anything were better than fewer numbers. The Yanks couldn't kill them all.

Joshua's right hand trembled when he checked the load in his Sharps carbine.

Cracks of rifle fire sounded from the hill. With the summer sun bearing down, he wiped the sweat from his forehead with his left hand. The hazy humid sky was further blurred by repeated bursts of gray smoke that rose from the Federals' big guns.

The regiment marched to about forty yards from the road that cut through the field when a blast from a cannon seared through the haze. It hit twenty yards in front of the right flank, spitting soil into the air that poured down like dirty rain. Joshua grabbed his cap and lowered his head to protect his eyes. While his left ear was ringing, another blast exploded on the left. Two men were lifted off their feet and then slammed back to the ground. Through his left ear, he heard a piercing scream followed by a wailing groan.

Fear gripped Joshua's chest. He wanted to turn back, but his legs carried him onward, as if they could think apart from his brain.

Twenty yards to the road.

More Yank cannon fire sent clumps of ground flying everywhere. With the sky so clouded with smoke, Joshua squinted to find the flag. He caught a glimpse, but then down went the flag as another blast hit the center of the line. Seconds later, the blue cross sprang straight up again.

"Prepare to fire!" shouted the regiment commander.

Joshua moved his rifle from shoulder rest to firing position. His shaking fingers tried to drop a ball into the barrel. It missed and bounced off his shoe. Then he remembered that he had already loaded.

Ten yards to get to the road.

"Fire at will!"

Shots rang out from thousands of Rebel guns. More Yank artillery splintered the ground in return. The ringing in his ears now throbbed through the top of his head. His steps slowed a pace. He tried to spit out the fear that had dropped into his belly, but his mouth could gather no saliva. He swallowed. What felt like slivers of broken glass slashed the inside of his throat.

Joshua stopped. Pointing his gun at the hill, he pulled the trigger. For an insane second, he believed his one shot would drive every bluebelly off the hill.

"Carter's down!" hollered somebody.

Joshua glanced to his right. Waterson was kneeling on the ground trying to hold what was left of Carter's right arm to the man's shoulder. Carter was breathing heavy and quick. His eyes, black and wide as saucers, looked up directly to the sky. Joshua bent down next to Waterson. Carter opened his mouth to speak between gasps of air. "Ya ain't gettin' me, ya devil bastards!"

"Hold on, Carter. We'll get you back safe," said Jenkins who had come up from behind.

Carter shifted his eyes toward Joshua. "Ya gotta kill those devil bastards," he said. "Don't aim ta hurt; aim ta kill!"

"I will," Joshua promised with an obvious uncertainty in his voice.

Waterson, with blood spilling over his hands, let go of Carter's arm—and it dropped off his shoulder onto the field. A river of blood gushed from the ghastly hole in his shoulder.

Joshua pointed to another dark stain under Carter's belt, so large that his pants were soaked red to his knees. More Yankee cannon fire blasted the field. Carter lifted the only hand he had left and put it to his throat. His body arched off the ground for a second before settling back onto the field.

Somehow, Joshua's hands managed to reload his gun as the sky exploded all around. In between the shells and the ringing in his ears, he could still hear horrible screams and groans from both sides of the line. His legs buckled, yet he walked on. He could barely see the flag through the smoke.

He got to the road. Several men were climbing over the fence. Two were shot as they did so and fell backward. The odor of burning flesh filled his nose, a stench he'd smelled only once before but would never forget as long as he lived. He lifted his left leg over the fence. When he rested his backside at the top, he saw a layer of men lying on the ground at the other side. One was a boy, curled up like a ball and weeping. His body was convulsing, and his face was frozen in fear. When Joshua jumped down, he nearly stepped on the boy's head. After he took a few steps, he looked behind and saw Jenkins trying to raise that boy up to his feet, but the boy would have none of it. Jenkins dropped him back down, and the boy curled right back up into a ball again.

The cry, "Keep going, Virginia!" sounded through the billowing smoke.

The command came from the left center of what was no longer a line. Joshua lost sight of the flag, but then he saw a general's hat pointing up from the top of a rifle. As he stepped toward the hat, he could hear an artillery shell whistling toward him. He dropped to the ground and covered his head with his hands. The shell hit to his right. The ground shook, and his body bounced up and then back down. Another bolt of pain shot through his head. He opened his eyes, and for a moment, he saw nothing but black. The ringing in his ears had muted the sounds around him, but he could still make out a soldier's cry from just ahead.

Joshua crawled forward. Waterson lay on his back, twisting and groaning, his mangled right leg burning in flames several feet away from his body. His organs spilled out onto the field from a long split in his belly. Joshua reached for his hand. Waterson glanced up at him before he shifted his eyes to the sky. He squeezed Joshua's hand once and then let go.

Rising to his feet, Joshua tried to steady his buckling knees. His head swelled with a new pain. So much smoke filled the air now that he could no longer tell which direction to go. Another shell hit closer, knocking him back down, ripping his rifle out of his hand. He got back up, stumbling in a circle. With no rifle to be found, he reached into his pocket for Becky's letter.

Joshua hobbled in some direction. His brain tried to think, but with his heart beating so fast, fear drove away any sensible thought. His eyes burned from the smoke. He stepped forward, and his foot sank into what he thought to be the belly of a fallen soldier. Rubbing the smoke from his eyes, he looked down.

Jenkin's face was half-gone. An empty black hole was left from where his right eye should have been. His mouth was twisted wide open. Joshua tried to lift him up and shake him back to life.

His mind cleared for a moment, and he remembered what Jenkins had said to him that morning. As he let his friend's body back down to the ground, Joshua cried out, "See you on the other side!"

He staggered away, coughing up smoke from deep inside his lungs.

Stumbling into a clearing, he could see again. A new breeze cooled his face. He scanned the field, trying to find Ol' Oakie.

"Becky! Becky, are you here?" He looked behind him. "Jenkins, help me find Becky!"

Somehow, Joshua had made it to the top of the hill.

"Becky! I'm right here. Don't you see me? I'm right here!"

On the crest of the hill, about ten yards off, he saw a rifle pointed straight at him. Behind the stock of the gun stood a bearded bluebelly.

"Where are you, Becky?"

Through another gap in the smoke, he caught a closer glimpse of the Yank. The Rebel Code of Honor flashed across Joshua's mind.

Never let them shoot you in the back. Never turn and run.

He moved one step forward. A new breeze swept across his face.

"Becky? Are you here?" Joshua looked behind him. Still no Jenkins. Then he stepped forward again. He blinked his eyes twice and saw Ol' Oakie standing tall on the crest of the hill. His eyes dropped down to a brilliant gold circle around his feet. He looked up again into a field of gleaming wheat waving in the wind.

Through the golden blaze, the Yank peered over his rifle.

The breeze swirled again. The fresh air soothed Joshua's burning lungs. He blinked his eyes again. The Yank seemed so close now that Joshua could reach out to shake his hand. Then in an instant, the Yank was gone, and he saw Becky standing on the hill in her blue dress with the yellow flower in her hair and that perfect smile on her face.

The crack of a rifle jolted Joshua away from Becky's smile. The ball struck him in the middle of his chest, knocking him backward. He tried to stay on his feet, but his legs collapsed inward, and he fell to the ground. The back of his head rested against a cool patch of grass. He gazed up at a beautiful blue sky.

With his final breath, Joshua stared into a brilliant white sun before everything faded to black.

Gettysburg Battlefield
July 4 – 5 p.m.

Rain pelted the field.

With scarves tied over their noses to keep out the stink of rotting human flesh, two Union soldiers tossed Confederate bodies into a shallow ditch. As they threw the next body into the hole, a piece of paper dropped from the dead man's hand. One of the Yanks stooped down and picked it up. A large green leaf fell out of the paper onto the ground.

"What's it say?" asked the other.

"Can't really tell. Most of it's rubbed out from the wet mud. It starts with 'Dear Parky.' That's about all I can make out."

"Well, whether it be a letter written to someone or a letter received, it don't matter no more. Throw it in the hole."

Coca-Cola Park, Allentown, Pennsylvania
June 22, 2008 – 9:45 p.m.

The umpire raised his right hand with the final out call, sending the Buffalo Bison back to his dugout. Dan slumped into his seat and pulled down his New York Mets baseball cap to just above his eyes.

Mary Jo sat up. "It's about time. I would rather stick a rusty nail through my eyeball than have to watch another inning," she declared.

"Are there fireworks now, Daddy?" Katy tugged on Dan's shirtsleeve.

He looked over at Jacob. "C'mon, son. Two on, nobody out, and they can't get one home to tie it up."-

"I was hoping for extra innings," Jacob said.

Mary Jo tried to open her mouth, but Jacob's words jumped out first.

"What, Mom? We came here to watch the Mets' minor leaguers play a baseball game."

"He's right," Dan added. "Fireworks are for the Fourth of July."

"You and your father came here to watch a baseball game. Your sister and your mother came here to see fireworks. We waited three hours for a fifteen-minute show." Mary Jo glared at Dan. "Jacob, don't get like your father, who's certainly old enough to know better. It's not always about what *you* want."

She pinched their son on his cheek.

Dan squeezed his mouth shut. Old enough, or just old? Yesterday, the cashier at the grocery store had patted Katy on the head and said, "That's so nice of you to help your grandpa bag the groceries."

Dan had snapped a look at Mary Jo. She had stood behind him, searching her purse for her wallet.

Katy had bagged the arthritis cream he needed for his sixty-year-old joints before she had tossed in Mary Jo's tanning lotion for her forty-year-young skin.

Of course, with two decades of separation between their ages, Dan expected some bumps in the road. After all, he had already been married six months to his first wife on the day Mary Jo took her first breath into her new world.

Do the math, they all said.

Dan's friends had tried to convince him she was young enough to be his daughter, and Mary Jo was warned not to marry a man older than her father.

On their wedding day, guests at the reception placed bets next to the flaming Cherries Jubilee. Odds favored this May-December thing was doomed. Some said give it six months, others gave it a year, but like that snowball's chance in hell, here they were now, fifteen years later, and all bets were off.

"I married you because I wanted a mature man who would understand and support me and not have me give up my ambitions just because you're done living your life," she'd told him the last time they had argued.

"Take care of the kids. Clean the house. Be with me. That's all you need to do, Mary Jo. My pension pays for everything. What the hell else is there for you to want? You're lucky I'm not one of those guys your age who sits around playing video games and drinking beer every friggin' day."

"I don't give a damn about your pension, Dan. And I'm not your babysitter or your cleaning lady." She scowled at him. "You're right about the video game guy, but *he* would let me do what I want because he wouldn't give a crap." Mary Jo raised her voice. "I *have* to get out of this house and do something with my life. I will get certified to be a nutritional health counselor so I won't have to depend on your money!"

"That'll be good," he told her. 'You can take better care of me."

"No, Dan. I'm taking care of *me*. I'm preparing for my life after you."

"Life after me is called 'insurance.' There's plenty of money for you and the kids."

"Oh good," she fired back. "You'll be dead, and I'll be dancing in the streets throwing hundred-dollar bills up in the air."

"A thousand women your age would change places with you in a second, and you know it."

"And they'd all run away once they'd see you have locks on the doors and bars on the windows in this prison of a house."

Mary Jo always had the last word, and each time she stormed from the room, she trademarked her exit with the slam of a door.

Dan tried to understand her frustration with him. One night, instead of battering him with her usual sarcasm, she threw tissues at him filled with her tears. That scared him into thinking that winning their arguments would mean losing her for good. That age thing, though, put up a no-vacancy sign in his brain. His body was telling him that the years he had left could be reduced to hours on the clock any day now. He wanted to enjoy what they could do together before it was too late.

Getting old scared the hell out of him—scared him so much he had nightmares of Mary Jo wiping the drool off his chin while Jacob and Katy rushed their friends past their decrepit old father sitting at the kitchen table in his underwear.

Yet he kept telling himself he was only sixty, the new fifty these days. *Relax. Be patient. Stop looking in the mirror.*

June 22 – 10 p.m.

Dan never told anyone he wasn't a fan of fireworks. He might as well as said he hated Santa Claus and the Easter Bunny, too. He would pretend to enjoy them now for the sake of the kids, but he knew the sight-and-sound show would bother him in a vague, uncertain way.

He leaned forward in his seat.

"Get ready! Here they come!" Mary Jo announced.

The first blast invaded the black sky with long ribbons of blue, white, and gold fire, followed by a series of loud cracks and booms.

From the onset of the explosions, Dan winced from a sharp pain in his head. His body lurched against the back of his seat. More explosions in the sky volleyed back and forth between his ears. Cannon fire pounded his chest. Gunshots rattled his temples.

"What's the matter?" Mary Jo asked, leaning over Jacob, who never took his eyes off the sky.

Dan looked over at her, surprised that she was even there. He forced a smile. "Oh, nothing, nothing. You know me. I've never liked loud noises."

Another launch sent a cascade of purples, greens, and reds beyond the centerfield scoreboard, followed by the next wave of smoky explosions.

Dan gripped the arms of his seat with both hands. He squeezed his eyes shut and lifted his body upwards before lowering himself back down as if he was dropping himself into a tub filled with ice.

Skies smoked. Voices screamed. Soldiers fell from a hail of bullets.

Dan twisted again from the next fiery blast over the scoreboard. He covered his ears with both hands and lifted his knees up to his chin. He tried to blink away the hurricane of horrors from inside his head.

In the center of the eye of the storm, a boy's frightened face appeared from beneath the cap of a Confederate Civil War soldier.

June 22 – 11 p.m.

With the kids asleep in the back seat of the car, Dan cued "Born on the Bayou" in the CD player. As he reached to pump up the volume, Mary Jo grabbed his wrist. "What the hell went on back there? You looked like you were having a seizure."

He looked at her, with that same face he'd worn at the game, as if she was a stranger who had wandered into the passenger seat of his car. "Oh, were you speaking to me? Sorry. Yeah, I'm okay, in case you should ask." Dan glared out at the open road.

Mary Jo turned off the music. "What happened to you with the fireworks?"

"I told you. I don't like the sound of gunshots."

"Gunshots? What gunshots?"

Dan opened his mouth to reply, but no words came out. He took a deep breath. "Mary Jo, I'm not really sure what happened or why it happened, and I sure as hell don't know what to do about it all."

"Talk to me, Dan."

He turned the music back on. He had control now. *She's concerned. She's worried. She's angry. All good,* he thought. He started to sing out of tune.

"And then I was just a little boy standin' to my daddy's knee. Born on the bayou. Born on the baaaaayoooo."

Mary Jo reached over and shut off the music again.

"Dan. Tell me what the hell is going on."

He took another deep breath and gripped the wheel with both hands. Time to get real. "I . . . saw this face."

"Where? Who? Someone at the game?"

"No. Someone in my head." Dan arched his back, flipping his high beams at an oncoming car. "Blond curly hair sticking out of the sides of his cap. Big blue eyes. Young. In fact, nineteen years young."

"So you saw the face of a nineteen-year-old kid in your head? In a cap? What kind of cap?"

"Confederate army," Dan said, as if he expected her to argue his answer. "A nineteen-year-old Confederate soldier."

"Oh, so he was wearing a gray hat, I think—or was it blue? I don't remember what side wore what color. How did you know he was nineteen?"

"That's the weirdest part," he replied, as if everything else made sense. "I wondered about his age, and the year '1844' flashed like a neon sign inside my head."

"He was nineteen in 1844?"

"No. He was born in 1844. He was nineteen in 1863."

"So in your head you saw this kid from the Civil War. And there were gunshots. Did you see someone shooting, too?"

"They were shooting at all of us," said Dan, suddenly realizing what he had said. "I mean him."

"Why did you just say 'us'?"

She was locked into his story. He felt it would be a relief to totally come clean.

"I don't know. I know this sounds crazy, but I was there. I was walking with his footsteps, in his shoes. He, I mean I was shot, and I believe I was killed."

Now he knew what she was thinking: *Dan the cynic, Dan the sceptic.* At Gary Miller's party in April, she'd had to yank him out the door. Gary had talked about a five-year-old kid who could play Beethoven without ever having a lesson. Dan called the kid a genius. Gary said the boy was a reincarnation of the original. A half-dozen rum and Cokes later, Dan stuck his jaw in his friend's face. "If someone was a born-again spider, well, too bad," he slurred. "I just squashed his head on your bathroom floor with my big-ass foot. What da ya say about that, Mr. Reincarno Man?"

A quick goodbye at the door and home they went. Mary Jo spent the next two days avoiding Dan whenever he came near.

"Why 1863?" she asked now.

Oh my God, Dan thought, *she held back her usual Assault with Deadly Sarcasm.*

"Because he . . . I was there fighting in the battle."

Mary Jo knew more about dead spiders than she did about nineteenth century American history. She sat back, probably deciding what question to ask next. Dan braked at a red light. He reached over and grabbed her wrist, squeezing a jolt of pain onto her face. He answered her next question before she could ask it.

"The Battle of Gettysburg."

June 23 – After Midnight

After they arrived home, Dan hurried to his laptop. Mary Jo went upstairs to put the kids to bed. At about two thirty, he heard footsteps on the stairs.

"You left the outside floodlight on," she said. "I thought you might be playing soldier, shooting your air rifle at enemy squirrels." Mary Jo sneered across the room at him, a look that thickened the air.

He forced up a cough.

"You could fill the bags under your eyes with groceries, Dan. What are you doing?"

He ignored her question, but then again, he knew she expected he would, having once told him that he had made a habit of placing her importance in the same category as the porcelain rabbits sitting in front of the family room fireplace.

She turned to leave.

"I have been trying to find a photo of his face," he said. "No luck. Not many pictures were taken of Confederate soldiers at Gettysburg, and those I found were photographs of corpses, most without their faces showing." Dan scratched his head. "I believe he was from Alabama."

"Have you considered the possibility that your vision was a figment of your imagination?"

"Mary Jo, listen to me. So much makes sense to me now. My favorite music is Southern rock, and my favorite writers are Twain and Faulkner. *Boy's Life*, my favorite novel, takes place in Alabama. I root for any baseball team from the South that makes it to the College World Series. Hell, when I was a kid I asked for a football helmet for Christmas. I wanted a red one with a white stripe down the middle because that was the helmet worn by the Alabama Crimson Tide, coached by Paul "Bear" Bryant. Then, when I coached high school football, what nickname did my players give me? The Bear! Don't you see the connections?"

"Oh, come on, Dan! You've lived your whole life in New Jersey, and now you're in Pennsylvania. You root for the New York Mets, the New York Giants, and the New Jersey Devils. You went to Charleston *once*, and unless you count Disney World, you have never even seen the South."

"I've always had a fascination with the Civil War. I read books. Studied battlefield maneuvers. Remember the time I got upset because the government ruled the Southern states couldn't fly Confederate flags at public buildings?"

"And I told you it was offensive to the descendants of slaves."

"Right. Of course, I get that. But what about all the men who died fighting for that flag? They were Americans who made the supreme sacrifice. Throw away the flag, and you throw away their legacies and make their lives meaningless."

"Let's not do this again." Mary Jo shook her head. "I am *not* going to argue politics at this God awful time of the morning."

Dan rubbed his tired eyes. "Come to think of it, when I was in Charleston many years ago, I visited a plantation. I had a weird feeling of comfort there. I've been in places like that before."

"So what the hell are you saying?" She raised her voice. "You saw this kid soldier in your head. The fireworks must have reminded you of a war movie, or something you saw in a magazine."

"No. No. No! This kid was in no movie. He fought at Gettysburg—that much I'm sure about. I was there. I remember the terrain." Dan leaned back in his chair. "If I could only know his name . . . "

"Don't forget that you have two children whose names are Jacob and Katy, who need a ride to school tomorrow. I have my nutrition class in Morristown. I'll be gone all day."

Dan glared at her over the top of the laptop screen.

"My kids? We have kids? Well, thanks for reminding me. You know I'm at that age now. Alzheimer's could be setting in."

He immediately wished he hadn't said that.

Then it came. Her smartass remark. "Keep looking for your dead soldier, Dan. If he pops into your head again, maybe this time he'll be wearing a red-and-white football helmet instead of a gray cap. Tell him to score me a touchdown." She turned and walked away.

Dan closed his eyes to accept some needed sleep, but his wide-awake mind returned him to that day of the red helmet.

⚬⚬⚬

A brisk September wind knifed through Danny's light brown jacket. At seven years old, it didn't take much to knock him off balance. Nevertheless, he had a football game to play—Alabama vs. Notre Dame.

With his Crimson Tide helmet strapped to his head, Danny threw the ball into the sky, pretending it was the opening kick-off. The white stripes on both points of the ball spiraled down into his hands. He took off as fast as he could, running across the backyard, dodging sticks, jumping over piles of leaves, racing for the end zone past the maple tree.

One Fighting Irish tackler to beat.

His dad's shirt flapped its sleeves from the clothesline. Danny lowered his head. He stiff-armed right through the middle of the shirt, snapping it off the line and sending it into a gust of wind.

"TOUCHDOWN!" he shouted to the low gray clouds. He took a knee under the snaps from the maple's applauding branches.

⚬⚬⚬

Hours into the early morning, Dan's sleep-starved body flinched when he heard Katy crying. After a comforting hug, he carried her back to his computer and sat her on his lap. Minutes later, he heard Mary Jo's feet stomping down the stairs.

"Hi, Mommy," said Katy, holding Biscuit, her stuffed dog.

Dan braced himself for her attitude he knew was coming next.

"Honey, what are you doing up?" Mary Jo asked while shaking her head at Dan.

Katy rubbed her eyes.

"I heard her cry, so I went up to her room," he answered. "She had a nightmare. She wanted me to stay with her for a while, so I brought her downstairs."

"Couldn't you have stayed in her room with her?"

"Daddy told me he's looking for a person on his computer."

"That's just fine, sweetie, but now it's time to get back into bed. You have school tomorrow. Come up with me, please."

"Okay, but can I tell Daddy something first?"

"Sure."

"Daddy, if you can't find your person on the computer, why don't you go meet him somewhere? "

Katy always found a way to simplify anything complicated. He let out a laugh, expecting Mary Jo's impatience to morph into anger. She took Katy by the hand. As they turned to leave, Dan jumped out of his chair.

"Wait a minute! Katy, I think you have something there." He straightened his back. Half of his brain was excited about finding Johnny Rebel, but the other half was swinging this dead soldier story by a single thread that was now holding his marriage together.

"Mary Jo, didn't your sister say she knew some guy, a hypnotherapist who specializes in, what's it called, past-life regression? That's it. You know, when you're under hypnosis, you can reconnect with a soul you know from a former life?"

She opened her mouth to speak, but he kept going with another rush of emotion or adrenalin or whatever it was that was keeping him awake.

"Remember? She told us what her friend had found out from this guy. He lived in Nazi Germany and was killed in the bombing of Berlin." Dan hurried over to Katy. He lifted her above his head before planting a kiss upon her forehead. "You're right, little guppy. Maybe I can meet Johnny Rebel." He put her back down.

Mary Jo, "I need to call your sister."

Dan reached for his cell phone on the table next to his laptop.

"Whoa!" Mary Jo rushed to grab his phone. "Are you kidding me? It's four o'clock in the morning. Have you lost your mind?"

The words froze them both for a moment.

"You're right," Dan said. "It's either too late, or it's too early. I'll call her at seven before she leaves for work."

"You have to drive the kids to the bus stop for eight o'clock. And if Katy doesn't get to sleep right now, she may be too tired to go. Then she stays home with you."

Dan returned to his laptop. He sighed, knowing that Mary Jo would leave for her class in the morning, relieving them both of each other. He wanted to shout, "I love you," but before his words could come out, her voice surged from the top of the stairs:

"Never mind how tired I will be!"

June 23 – Mid-morning

Fueled by an adrenalin rush that was now in its twelfth hour, Dan drove to Bethlehem. Since connections to his vision of a past life continued to multiply, why not add another to the count.

His life as ten-year-old Danny Bryant had never been so intriguing. As a shy boy surviving the miseries of a house on Desna Street in Piscataway, New Jersey, he had learned that anything he wanted in life he'd have to get on his own.

∞

"You tell that coach of yours you're tired of sitting on the bench!" yelled his father, lining up bottles of Seagram's whiskey and Budweiser beer on the kitchen counter. "You tell him you're better than that puny good-for-nothing they got playing second base."

"But, Dad, I can't do that. He won't listen to me. Can you talk to him?"

His father drained a shot of whiskey, followed by a belt from a beer. "You're old enough to stand up for yourself, boy. You tell him on Monday."

After practice on Monday, Danny shuddered as he tapped Coach Jerry on the back of his hip.

"What can I do for you, little man?"

"Can I try out for second base?"

Coach Jerry laughed so loud the rest of the team spun their bicycles around to see what was going on. "We got a second baseman. Tommy's nothing much with the glove, and he *has* been slumping lately." Jerry looked down at Danny and shrugged. "Get your glove and get out there."

Danny fielded the first dozen or so balls without error before one got under his glove. Then he swept up the next half bucket of balls, ranging far from his left to his right.

"It's late. Time to go," hollered Coach Jerry from home plate.

The next day, Danny started at second base. He made two clean fielding plays and smacked two base hits. Each game, he got better and better. At the end of the season, he was selected for the town's All Star team.

"Didn't I tell you?" his dad said.

And that was it. Dad never came to watch him play a single inning, other than a year before when Danny came off the bench for the last two innings of a game and dove to make a one-handed catch of a line drive hit toward right center field.

In the All Star game, Danny ripped a double off the centerfield wall to drive in two runs. When he got home that night, he walked right past his father, who was watching television. When Danny skipped down the hall, he took a phantom swing and hit that pitch again, watching the imaginary ball bounce off the ceiling.

Baseball and rock music saved him from his own childhood.

Most nights Danny locked himself in his room cranking out the music of Creedence, Deep Purple, Santana, and the Guess Who on his high-fidelity stereo. After dinners, he hurried back to pretend he was singing with Tommy James and the Shondells or riffing chords off his air guitar with Mark Farner and Grand Funk Railroad. No matter how hard he tried to escape the brawls between his mother and father, their hatred toward each other scared away any chance he might have had to be a happy kid.

One night when he was twelve and his older sisters had moved out of the house, Mom and Dad came home drunk from a neighbor's party.

"Your mother is a goddamn whore!" Dad yelled at Danny.

"I shoulda listened to my mother," Mom said, slamming her beer glass onto the table. "She told me not to marry a no-good nothing like you!"

And they were off to throwing punches of drunken insults for fifteen rounds.

Danny lay in bed with his pillow wrapped around his ears that night. He needed to hate them both to block the tears from flooding his eyes, but after he heard Dad smash a bottle on the kitchen table and his mother scream, he couldn't help but cry.

Mom fired a deathblow at Dad, reminding him that he'd gone out drinking with his boys the night she gave birth to "the only son you'll ever have!"

"We shoulda had rabbits instead of kids!" slurred Dad. A moment later, Mom stumbled down the hall, sobbing and bouncing from wall to wall until Danny heard her disappear through their bedroom doorway.

He wanted to get up to hug her. Instead, he threw his pillow across the dresser at the foot of his bed, knocking his New York Mets bobblehead doll to the floor where it shattered into pieces.

June 23 – Around Noon

Bethlehem, Pennsylvania, was an old steel city about thirty miles outside Dan's home in Jim Thorpe. For him, the downtown Main Street of retail shops, office buildings, and boutique eateries would be the center of what he hoped would be his moment of reckoning. His imagination compared this pilgrimage here to the journey one family took to that other Bethlehem, where a miraculous birth changed the way millions of people understand life and death.

He was about to do the same thing for himself. He thought the saga of the young soldier could be the center of a story he'd write and gift to his children as an heirloom. Dan laughed aloud, thinking of calling it "A Rebirth in Bethlehem."

If this experiment worked, he wondered if he would ever be Dan Bryant again.

As he maneuvered an *S*-curve on Route 248, he replayed Mary Jo's voice just before he left.

"C'mon, Dan. Fireworks are gunshots from some battle that was fought so long ago nobody cares to remember? This must be some sign of dementia or mental illness. I was hoping you wouldn't go crazy until you at least reached seventy." She'd said it in a joking way, but he knew she wasn't kidding.

He had asked himself why liking her was so difficult yet loving her was never in question. Beyond her long blond hair and her voluptuous figure—even after birthing their two children—Mary Jo was spiritually engaging. As he made a right hand turn onto Indian Hill Road, he recalled their conversation about the existence of God.

"I don't get it. Why do some people have to attach the meaning of their lives to a Biblical word?" she asked. "They want God in their lives? Go get him. He's real. He's in people. He's in the lakes, and he's in the trees, too. I find it sad that the best someone can do is believe in him because of the printed words on the page of a book."

Dan loved her banter. Mary Jo's sex appeal dripped from her lips when she talked from her soul.

"So where, my love, should we look for God?" he asked. "Under a rock? In the back seat of the car? How about we look up into the sky?"

He was baiting her again, and she knew it. But she answered with resolution. "God can be anywhere, Dan. In the eyes of a child. Sitting on a tree branch. I can see God in you, too, but only after you cough up the devil from your throat."

They used to laugh after a remark like that, but now those kinds of words bit hard into his gut. Like two leaves floating together down a rolling stream until split apart by a huge boulder, Dan didn't know what it would take for the two of them to find each other again in calmer waters on the other side of that big rock.

His fate now summoned him to David Lotz, a hypnotherapist-slash-past-life-regressor who was about to delve into Dan's conscience, predicated upon a thirty-second phone call made at eight fifteen this morning.

Dan drove down the main drag in Bethlehem, counting the address numbers until he saw 357 Main Street, a tall office building sandwiched between a boutique and a jewelry store. He felt a bit nauseous thinking it was here that he might travel back to the 1860s. He tried to laugh away the gurgle in his gut, thinking that after the session, he and David Lotz might walk across the street to Starbucks, sip lattes, and plan a new attack at Gettysburg, a strategy that this time would deliver the victorious Army of Northern Virginia back home to their loved ones.

He found Lotz's nameplate attached to a door on the third floor. He walked into a dark, small room. Three candles illuminated a desk with an open laptop. A black recliner was situated into the left corner. Soft piano music played from an iPod fixed upon a silver speaker. As he was taking this in, a rear door opened, and a heavyset, middle-aged man waddled into the room. He stood sort of slumped, his belly stuffed inside a striped shirt that was losing its battle to stay tucked in his pants. Swollen cheeks bulged below two slits for eyes. His top and bottom lip formed a smile with some effort before they returned to what appeared to be a nearly perfect circle.

"Good morning. I'm David Lotz. You must be Dan Bryant— or should I call you Johnny Reb?" He laughed in a voice coated with a throaty congestion.

"That's me," said Dan, adjusting his baseball cap. He laughed at Lotz's remark, but it was more like an eighth grade boy's nervous chuckle after bumping into the freshman hottie in the hall.

"Glad to meet ya," said Lotz. "Before we get started, I'd like to get to know ya, a piece from the personal side, if ya don't mind. But keep the bullshit to a minimum. I got another client comin' in at one. You can leave your sex life out too, unless ya brought pictures. Your sister-in-law did show me a pic of your wife. She is eeeeassy on the eyes, I'll tell ya that for sure."

"Thanks for the compliment," Dan said, in a sarcastic response Mary Jo would have admired. A moment of awkward silence pervaded the room until Dan figured it was his turn to speak next. "Will this session determine if I'm certifiable or not?" Another junior high school laugh escaped his mouth.

"Hell, aren't we all?" Lotz bellowed.

Dan thought of asking about the man's credentials or experiences with hypnotherapy since he had no licenses or certifications on the walls.

"I see you're looking for my diploma," the fat man said. "Well, I don't believe in the hypocrisy of spending lots of money for a piece of paper that's worth nothing more than to be used to line the bottom of a bird cage." Lotz told Dan that his training came from several visits to a psychic lady. "It was powerful, ya know? Her spirits grabbed me by my testicles and shook them so hard I got their message, all right. She taught me how to help people dig out the shit they have crammed inside their heads. In fact, I've been thinking of changing my nameplate to Doctor Laxative."

This time Lotz's laugh evolved into a phlegm-rising cough, making him grab for a handkerchief from his pocket.

With a growing sense of discomfort, Dan asked if hypnotherapy provided a decent living in return.

"Of course not. I'm a limo driver. I just do this as a side job."

Nausea gripped the inside of Dan's stomach again. He excused himself to use the bathroom located down the hall next to the psychiatrist's office. Good to know that. The psycho room just might be his next stop after his session with this fraud was over.

Dan returned from the bathroom with a different perspective about Lotz. *What the hell?* he thought. There is no worst-case scenario here. If Doctor Laxative pushed nothing out of him, Dan needed no other reason to go back to the business of being a husband and a father. He fell into the recliner feeling a new sense of peace.

"Comfortable enough?" Lotz asked. "Would you prefer I leave the soft music?"

"How about playing "Keep on Chooglin'" by Creedence Clearwater?" Dan was glad he said that.

"Shit yeah! CCR." Lotz broke into the song with a pretty good John Fogerty voice. "'Here come Louie, works in the sewer. He gonna choogle tonight.' We play that song, and there might be some honeys from this office hole come in here, take off their shoes, and start shakin' their butts in this here candlelight."

Mr. David Lotz, alias Doctor Laxative, now seemed right for this event, which was taking on an aura of genuine hocus-pocus. A limo driver was better than a book-smarty with a doctorate degree hanging around his neck. Another plus. If the whole matter flushed down the toilet, Johnny Reb would be erased forever by a glorified taxi driver-slash-hypnotherapist. How good would that be?

"So give me a summary of your life. Your sister-in-law said you're sixty-two years old?"

"Sixty," said Dan.

"Damn. So you must have married a younger woman for the sex, and she married you for the money."

"Yeah, something like that," Dan sighed, "but there's not much of either anymore." He was happy he said that too for the truth of it and for the ongoing ease he was building with Lotz.

Dan then rambled out a synopsis of his life. "I was born to parents who fell in love in Hazleton, Pennsylvania. I had a pathetic childhood, unless you count my Little League baseball career . . . I was a helluva player. My coaches were amazed at my hand-eye coordination. I could hit anything a pitcher threw at me if I swung. I once had twelve base hits in a row. The high school coach told me I was a shoe-in to play for a big-time college until the accident happened."

"The accident?" asked Lotz.

"I was playing third base in my first varsity game, and the batter hit a foul pop-up to my right. I took off after it, paying no attention to the bleachers. I reached for the ball and tripped. My face caught the bottom wooden corner. I rolled over. No pain at first. Then I heard Jimmy Flint, our shortstop, throwing up."

"What happened?"

"The batter was out. I caught the ball."

"To your face."

"Fractured eye socket. Doctor said I came within a millimeter of the bone piercing the back of my eyeball. No surgery, but the splintered bone would stay there like that forever. He told me I was done with baseball. Any further injury to the area and I could go blind."

"Tell me about your dad."

"Once we went on a fishing trip, and he stumbled head first into the lake after draining a flask of whiskey. Our father-and-son bonding had as much of a chance as a salmon does jumping over a waterfall.

"His unemployment led to welfare. We tried to survive in a small town called New Market, later to be named Piscataway in New Jersey. My parents crawled inside whiskey bottles and never came out. My sisters moved away. Dad died of multiple problems when I was a student at Rutgers. Mom lamented her woulda-shoulda-coulda life. She lived on booze and buttered bread until her fourth heart attack took her out at age seventy-five."

Dan smirked. "We were raised to believe that an occasional sunny day would be followed by weeks of straight rain," he said, thinking that if Mary Jo were here, she would tell him to get over his pity party.

He locked his hands together behind his head and leaned the recliner back as far as the chair would go. "Any time I would tell my mother something good about my life, she seemed disinterested. Tell her about a bad day, and her ears perked, and she could chirp for hours about her arthritis giving her pain or her huge fuel bills. It always ended with nobody cared about her, yada yada yada."

Dan was distracted for a moment by the groan at the bottom of Lotz's chair.

"My dad was always sick with something," he continued. "When he got emphysema added to his problem with restless legs, he had so much trouble breathing he couldn't sleep or sit. He leaned on the backs of chairs, always huffing and puffing. Of course, being a teenager at the time, I didn't feel compassion, just anger. We never could do anything together. No baseball. No trips anywhere. Once I begged him to play catch with me at the park. He drives me there, and after walking to the field, he's so out of breath he lies down right next to the seesaw and falls asleep. People walk by asking me if he needs an ambulance. I was so damn embarrassed.

"Then, on the drive home, he falls asleep at the wheel. The car's going off the road and I yell, 'Dad!' and he opens his eyes and yanks the car back onto the road. He swings his arm and cracks me right across my chest. That's the thanks I got for saving our lives."

"So your mom was a whiner," Lotz said. "Your dad was a zombie. You were married before. What about the first wife?"

Dan was enjoying David's insensitivity.

"You know how it goes," said Dan. "At first, hormones and testosterone lead you to believe that even after ten years of marriage, you'll still be having sex on the dining room table."

Lotz belched out a laugh.

"Then, when we decided to make money and not have kids, our relationship, well, it got kind of sour, and not only was there no sex on the dining room table; we never even ate dinner there. I guess you could say that once the fires of passion burned out, we lost interest in even talking to each other."

"So you went from a porn star wannabe to the invisible man."

"That's one way of putting it, I guess. I think I went from Jay Gatsby to a dead man walking. It was a disaster until we sat down one day and decided to separate. You know how that works out." Dan paused to think. "Funny thing was we never argued or yelled at each other, as I do now with Mary Jo." Dan glanced at Lotz to remind himself he wasn't down the hall in the psychiatrist's office.

Lotz swung around in his chair to lower the volume of the piano music. "That's because you didn't care enough to give a shit about the first wife, but now it's different," said Lotz, leaning back in the chair, which groaned in anguish. "When you love hard, you fight hard."

Dan liked that. Lotz was already validating. Maybe he really was a shrink in disguise. "You telling me the truth that you just drive a limo?" Dan asked.

"The automobile is a great place to play head games on long trips." His laugh struggled through another gurgling cough. "You wouldn't believe some of the shit I hear from the back seat on those long rides to the airport."

He glanced at his watch. "Okay, we better get started. Let's see if Johnny Rebel shows himself."

David Lotz pulled the switch to operational mode.

"First, let me tell ya that I ain't swingin' no watch and chain in front of your face," he said. "That shit's for circuses and boardwalk biddies. You will not lose present reality for one minute. You will have full awareness of this room, and you will hear noises from in here or from out in the hallway."

Dan twisted in the recliner. "So how does this work?"

"You'd better know that maybe it won't."

"What do you mean?"

"Some people can't leave their current state of consciousness, no matter how hard they might try."

"I'll give it my best shot."

Lotz leaned so far forward in his chair that Dan thought the bolts underneath would pop off onto the floor.

"The other thing is that even if you do get there, you might get a whole different result than what you're believing now. Couple weeks back, a woman thought she was some kinda princess in merry old England. She discovered she was a peasant girl who died from the plague before her fifteenth birthday."

"That's a pleasant change of stories," said Dan. "One more question, if you don't mind."

"Shoot."

"If Johnny Rebel does pop up, how do I know if he's real or I'm just making him up?"

"Oh, he'll be real all right if he comes from your alpha state of consciousness. That's where the mind stores all truth. You'll talk about details that you could never make up in such a rapid-fire way. This alpha will be your video screen. You'll watch a movie inside your head. We hypno guys call it the theater where the truth never lies.

"You see, we have the power to lie whenever we want to, *except* when we enter the alpha state. There the mind holds power over us. Just imagine if we lived inside the alpha state every day," Lotz continued. "You'd hear things like, 'Yes, dear, I *am* screwing our neighbor's wife,' or O. J. Simpson would have said, 'I killed them both,' and not wasted everyone's time with that joke of a trial."

"Is there any place other than this alpha consciousness where we can't lie?" Dan asked.

"There *is* one other place," said Lotz.

"Where's that?

"On our deathbeds. No need to be false to the world anymore when you're about to leave it."

Dan felt ready for anything, but he was really hoping this little experiment would end this fixation with the visions in his head, so he could get his mind back to Mary Jo and the kids.

"Sit back and relax. You'll need a lot of patience," said Lotz.

Dan followed his orders. He closed his eyes. He could hear Lotz's whispering voice above the piano music and below the clatter of footsteps in the hall.

"Relax your body. Relax your mind. Let everything go. Feel the peace. Feel the calm. Free your mind of everything."

At some point, which seemed to be at least an hour later, Dan was ready to give up. His mind wandered from what Mary Jo was planning for dinner to the chances of the New York Mets getting back to another World Series. Then, as if someone had conked him on the head with a hammer, he felt very sleepy.

Lotz went on with repeating his words over and over again. "Relax. If you should see something in your mind, tell me at once."

As if upon that cue, something bounced across Dan's mind, tumbling like dice tossed across a craps table.

I see something!

"What do you see?"

This something took form after spinning inside Dan's head. *It's a house! A house flying through the air, but now it's landing on the ground!* Dan had a quick reality check. How stupid he must be, thinking the house had flown from the sky to the ground, as Dorothy's did from *The Wizard of Oz!*

"What does this house look like?" asked Lotz.

Dan focused his mind's eye. *It's white with two big pillars in the front.*

"Does it have a door?"

Yes. It's wood like the house. Let me get closer. There's a door latch.

"Can you open the door and go in?"

Let me try. Yes! I just opened it. I'm going in. It's really big inside. High ceilings. Big windows. I can see through the glass right up to the sky.

"What about you? How old do you think you are?"

I'm not sure. Wait! I see a bedroom over to the right.

"Go into the bedroom and describe what you see."

I'm in here now. There's a small bed. Next to the bed is a wooden box. Let me see if I can open it. There are clothes here, shirts, pants with suspenders, and some shoes like the ones I'm wearing now. They're made from some kind of fabric or maybe an animal skin. They're like moccasins.

"Is this your room?" Lotz asked.

I don't know. Shouldn't I know?

"Come back out of the room. Tell me, what else do you see around the house?"

I'm in the big room again. I see two pictures on the wall. One is a man in a black suit. He has a long mustache and a few hairs of a beard on his chin. He looks serious and formal. Next to him is a picture of a woman. She's beautiful. She has dark hair underneath what looks like a white bonnet. She's wearing a long dress, and she's holding an umbrella over her right shoulder.

"Are these pictures of your mother and father?"

I don't know about him. I think she's my mother.

"Is there anything else in the room?"

I don't see—wait! There's someone here. He's a black man with a curly white beard. He's wearing gray overalls. He's got a friendly smile on his face.

"Do you know who he is?

Charles Joseph or Joseph Charles. Wait. Where did he go? He was just here smiling at me. He's not here anymore.

"Can you see what's in the back of the house?"

There's a door that leads out back. I think I know where it goes. I see a big field. I've been there many times before.

I'm walking outside through the field now. The wheat is so high it reaches my head. Oh, there's a huge tree off to the left. This is my tree. I call it Ol' Oakie. It's real tall, with really big limbs. There's moss hanging from some of the branches. I'm under Ol' Oakie now, looking straight up. The sun is coming down through the branches right on top of me. It's so beautiful here. I'm going to sit down now and lean my back against Ol' Oakie's trunk.

It's really hot. The air is still. It must be a summer afternoon. I'm looking across the field now. I thought for a second I saw some-one walking through the wheat, coming toward me. Yes! I see her now. She's smiling at me. She's pretty, too. Here she comes. She's really close now. I hear her calling someone's name.

"Joshua, Joshua Park. Is that you, Parky?"

Is that my name? Joshua Park? Now she's calling me Parky. Oh, she's saying her name is Becky.

Dan felt a sudden jolt when he heard voices talking in the hall.

Lotz's voice interrupted the distraction. "Anything else? Is Becky still walking toward you?"

This wonderful breeze just came from . . . somewhere. It's so cool and refreshing. I can feel it touch my face. I feel like closing my eyes, just taking it all in. It's so peaceful here. Becky is reaching her hand out to me now.

No! No!

"What's the matter?"

Where's Ol' Oakie? What happened to the breeze? Where did Becky go? She's gone. I'm not there anymore.

"Where are you?"

I'm standing in front of another field. I'm holding a gun! There are soldiers to my left and to my right. They're all holding guns. I don't want to be here. I'm scared. There are explosions all around me now. My ears are ringing!

Dan crawled up into a fetal position in the recliner. He covered his ears with his hands.

"Are you okay, Dan?" asked Lotz. "Do you want to continue, or should we stop here?"

Dan uncoiled his body.

We're marching up the field now. More explosions. Terrible smoke, too. Oh my God—

"Dan, should we stop now?"

No. No. I can't stop. I have to keep going. They're shooting at us. Bodies falling everywhere. There's no place to hide.

"Do you know where you are? Do you know these men?"

There's a hill up ahead. That's where we're going. Jenkins told me it's called Cemetery Ridge. "Right appropriate name," he said.

There's blood everywhere! Over here, I see one of my boys. He's missing an arm—it's Carter! I think he's dead. I have to climb over this damn fence. Everyone's going down. I see somebody crying; he's trying to crawl under the fence to hide. Oh my God, Waterson's down. His eyes aren't moving; they're looking straight up to the sky.

I'm on the other side of the fence now. I can't hear anything. The ringing in my ears. No! Somebody got shot down in front of me. It's Jenkins! He's my friend! Get up! Get up!

Smoke blinding me. Wait! Now I can see. There's a clearing. There's . . .

Dan paused suddenly.

"What do you see now?" asked Lotz.

I'm confused. I don't know where to go or what to do. I lost my gun somewhere. I'm holding a piece of paper in my hand. It's a letter from Becky. There's a soldier in blue. I'm so close I can see the hairs of his beard. He's pointing a gun right at me. Oh, there's a cool breeze blowing into my face. It feels good. I think I see Becky! Yes! She's right there at the top of the hill.

"Becky?"

I hear a gunshot! There's a bright white flash! My chest hurts bad. I'm on the ground. I can't breathe. I can't see. Everything is . . . is black.

Dan pulled his knees to his chest, squeezing his eyes shut.

"Okay, Dan. We'll stop right now. Can you hear me?"

Dan heard Lotz, but he couldn't stop gasping for breath. His body shivered in the recliner. "I'm cold," he said. "I'm . . . I'm dead."

"Not in this life you're not."

Lotz left the room and then returned to throw a blanket over Dan's quivering body.

Dan stopped shaking and sat up in the recliner. He looked over at Lotz, who sat rocking in his chair. Dan could think of only one question to push out through the buzz in his brain. "Can you explain to me what just happened?"

"That's not what I do," Lotz replied calmly. "Remember? I'm just a limo driver. You own this. You tell *me* what happened."

Dan tried to take a deep breath that hitched about halfway up. "I guess we can say that this is all real. I mean, I can't blame this on my imagination or just because I wanted it to happen."

"You were in alpha state," said Lotz. "You were telling the truth."

"Are you sure?"

"When the mind goes into a stream of consciousness like that, it's a purging of truth. Your details were vivid and quick. Conscious lying requires gaps of time for the mind to decide what to say next."

"He's real, then. I mean he was real." Dan swiped his hand across his head. "All of it's true. His age, Gettysburg, how he died." Dan sat back with his hands locked behind his head.

"I don't understand why I didn't remember about the house, and yet I knew about Joseph Charles and—and this girl, Becky, told me her name and told me my name, too. And the field with Ol' Oakie."

"Okay, my friend, I'll take my best shot to explain what I think," chimed Lotz. "Apparently, Johnny Reb, or Joshua Park, wants you to know some things but not others. He doesn't care to remember much about his home or his father, but he does want you to know about the good things, like Joseph Charles, Becky, and that field with the tree."

"What about the battle where he was killed?"

"All that too and the names of the soldiers, he wants you to know."

"But why me? Why him? What am I supposed to do with all this?"

"Ah. Those are your questions that still have to be answered."

"I mean, we might have some things in common, but there's no logic to why he chose me. What about that letter? How come I don't know what it says?"

Lotz leaned forward from his chair. He waited until Dan looked him in the eyes. "If you ask me, it's all about the babe," said Lotz.

"What do you mean?"

He smiled again and his eyes sank into his face. "These kinds of stories are always about the babe, my friend. Dan Bryant didn't die at Gettysburg," said Lotz. "He's sitting right here, right now, alive and kicking. Joshua Park is deader than dead, all right, but he's given you his little chickadee and a mystery about them that needs to be solved."

"He's cursed me with his pain and suffering. That's what he's done," said Dan, dropping his face into his hands.

"How 'bout you take it as a gift and not a curse." Lotz said, his eyes vanishing into his face again. "Of all the millions of people that have lived and died, you were chosen, my man, to be given his soul." Lotz laughed so hard the floor shook beneath him. "Now ain't that some shit to shovel at the wife when you get home!"

June 23 – 3 p.m.

Dan drove back to Jim Thorpe with more questions, more problems.

"What the hell just happened to me?" he asked aloud.

Something had rattled his brain at the baseball game, a mind-shock that manifested itself into an illogical truth. Yet Joshua Park's amazing journey from a plantation home to Gettysburg had stimulated every nerve in Dan's body. He talked out loud to the road ahead. "I didn't just see him. I was him. I am him."

What had made sense in the past with Dan's love for the South lost its significance in what now became a burden stuck inside his conscience. "Why does this happen when I'm sixty years old? Why not when I was much younger? How come I didn't know Joshua Park when I was a little kid? And what about the girl? Is there a new Becky somewhere going through this same damn thing I am?

"I need a battle plan," he said, tongue-in-cheek.

He would start by finding out about reincarnation to see if that might explain his two lives. He had asked about doing another hypnotherapy session; Lotz had told him they could try, but many times the anxiety for expecting more of the truth prohibited a second entrance into the alpha state.

A better idea popped into his head. "Go to Gettysburg." He had to say this aloud for self-conviction.

Exhaustion weighted his eyelids. Add it all up, and he was on his twenty-sixth hour with only fifteen minutes of sleep. He rubbed his eyes with the back of his hand. The search for an explanation would have to wait. He would get home, set the alarm to pick up the kids at the bus stop, take a nap, and have enough gas left in his tank when Mary Jo came back from New Jersey to explain to her what happened.

A squirrel ran out from the side of the road. With eyes half closed, Dan slammed on the brakes. As the car skidded to a stop, his body lurched forward with only the seat belt preventing his head from slamming into the windshield. After relaxing his hands on the steering wheel, he pressed on the gas pedal as if he was stepping on an egg. He turned onto Sweet Briar Lane toward his house at the end of the street.

Dan compared his life now to striking out in a baseball game.

Losing his own identity—strike one.

Losing his mind—strike two.

Losing Mary Jo to a ghost named Becky—strike three.

As he pulled into the driveway, he told himself he needed to sleep. Even if Robert E. Lee stood at his doorstep, he would salute the general, walk right past him, and go upstairs to bed.

June 23 – 4:15 p.m.

Dan opened his heavy eyes. He glanced at the clock next to his bed. "Shit," he shouted. He threw off the blanket. Fifteen minutes had passed since the bus would have dropped off the kids.

He heard the front door open. Pulling up his pants, Dan scampered down the stairs, nearly tripping on the last step.

"Dad, where were you?" Jacob asked, leaving the door open for Katy to enter.

"Sorry, son, I took a nap. I guess I didn't hear the alarm go off."

Jacob looked at Dan with the kind of disappointment on a child's face that no parent wants to see. "So, how was school today?" asked Dan, changing the subject. Jacob marched past him into the kitchen.

"Hi, Daddy!" shouted Katy. Dan could always count on his daughter's unconditional love. She ran in to his arms, and he gave her his welcome-home lift and kiss on her forehead.

"How's my little guppy?"

"Fantastic!"

At least he had a third of his family's love at the moment. He knew he'd win Jacob back. He hoped to reach 100 percent with Mary Jo at the dinner table.

∞

Mary Jo prepared a dinner of roast pork loin. She sat down at the kitchen table with a glass of cabernet at her fingertips.

Eating dinner was devoid of the usual conversations about the day's events. Dan could tell that Mary Jo had cued in on his tense silence. With his food nearly finished, Jacob's request broke through the clatter of forks and plates.

"Can I be excused? Jessie asked if I would play her in a game of soccer in her backyard."

Dan and Mary Jo were hearing a lot about Jessie, the pretty brown-haired girl who lived next door. She played Jacob in everything from checkers to soccer to Wiffle ball to Nerf-gun war. She was good at it all, too. They spent many afternoons arguing over who won or who cheated.

"It's a love-hate thing," Mary Jo had said with a laugh to Jessie's mother, Diana, at last weekend's backyard barbecue. "It's what teenagers do. I think they really like each other."

Dan had kidded with Jessie's father while he ate a cheeseburger. "You better save for the wedding, Mike."

"What, for the church reception hall? I got it covered."

"Do they have chandeliers and crystal glasses at the church hall?" Dan had asked.

"Last time I was there," said Mike, "most of the dust-covered light bulbs were still lit, and they got in a new supply of red Solo cups."

Jacob stood up to leave.

"You tell your girlfriend that there are still a few days left before school lets out, so you're expected home in an hour," said Mary Jo.

"Mom, she's not my girlfriend! I don't even really like her," Jacob protested. "She's just someone to hang with when nobody else is around."

Dan glanced at Mary Jo, who was trying her best to not laugh at Jacob's remark.

"Whatever you say, son," said Dan. "I'll tell Jessie's father the next time I see him that you're not saving your birthday money for the engagement ring just yet."

Jacob rolled his eyes and hurried from the room.

Katy lifted her fork from her plate. "Mommy, when Torrie's mom took us home today, she said Torrie and I could have a sleepover on Saturday. Can we?"

Mary Jo narrowed her eyes and fired a look over at Dan. "Torrie's mom took you home? Where were you, Dan?"

"When I got back from Bethlehem, I took a nap and forgot to set the alarm."

"Katy, dear," Mary Jo said, "you're excused. I need to speak with your father. We'll talk about the sleepover later."

Katy danced out of the kitchen. Dan could feel the air thicken as Mary Jo zeroed in for the interrogation. "So tell me. What happened in Bethlehem?"

Dan decided not to be careful with his words and just went with the truth. "Everything, honey. Everything happened. It's all true. My name was Joshua Park, and I had a girlfriend named Becky." He replayed his session with Lotz. His emotions got in the way a few times, so he had to backtrack to be sure he left out no details. When he finished his story, Mary Jo looked at him in a moment of silence, as if she were planning something dramatic to say.

"So can we now put this whole thing back into a story for Ripley's Believe It or Not?" she said in a tone of voice that spiked him in the groin.

"That's all you can say? Just put this whole thing away somewhere?" He picked up his pace now. "I'll tell you where I'll put this thing after I figure out what it all means." He slapped his hands upon the table. "This dead soldier from Alabama pushed his way into my brain for some obvious reason. He, or whoever put him in this world so many years ago, chose ME! He chose ME! Does that make any sense to you? There is no putting this anywhere else until I find out what the hell HIS life has to do with MY life!"

Dan's loud words fired a direct hit. He stopped to reload, which gave Mary Jo a chance to shoot back.

"How do you know that this kid ever existed at all? You talk about him as if the two of you are the same person, but then you tell me you can watch him in your mind as if he's somebody else. You make no sense, Dan." She walked to the sink and turned around. "How do you know that after you're done chasing his ghost, you won't end up in the nuthouse? HOW DO YOU KNOW I'm going to wait around for you to stop this silliness and become the man I married?" She stood up and jammed her chair into the edge of the table.

Dan knew he needed to pull back. "Mary Jo, I have been down that road of doubting this story. In fact, I wish that this damn thing never happened, but it did, honey. It did."

She began to leave the room but stopped to turn around. "So now what?" she demanded.

"I have to go to Gettysburg to see if there are any more clues."

"And what do you expect to find there? A hand waving from a grave at you, saying, 'I'm over here, Dan, the dead kid from the South who's now become you'? And what about me, Dan? You want me to be the idiot wife who follows behind you in the grocery store telling everyone, 'My husband is a Civil War soldier come back to life, and next October he's going to dress up in his uniform and join the Halloween parade in town'?"

"This isn't about you, Mary Jo."

"Exactly. It's never about me, is it, Dan? It's always about *you*. I'm supposed to forget my own stupid life and just think about the drama in *your* life. No, let me correct myself: in your TWO lives!" She turned toward Dan with her hand on her hip. "I have always worried how I was supposed to live with you when you got to be an old man. I guess that issue has come sooner than I expected." She turned to leave the room again, but Dan knew she wasn't finished with him yet.

"You just went from sixty to 150 years old in a matter of forty-eight hours," she snapped. "Let me know when you're leaving for Gettysburg. I'll whistle "Dixie" before you go."

A door slammed, and Dan got up from the table. From across the room, his eyes zeroed in on a bottle of Bacardi. After he'd drained a Coke-colored glass of rum, his mind jolted him back to a scene when he was eleven years old. He looked down at his hands and curled them around an imaginary baseball bat.

Danny waited on deck with his fingers crossed, hoping Joey would get a hit to win the game.

"Ball four, take your base," said the umpire.

As Joey trotted to load the bases, he glanced over at Danny. "C'mon," he said between his teeth. "You gotta come through this time!"

This time, Danny said to himself he would try not to think about his mother crying every night at the kitchen table with another beer in her hand. This time he wouldn't think about his dad, drunk and naked, beating against the back door that had locked him outside the house in the dark.

"Just be sure you get a good pitch to hit," coach had said.

With three balls and two strikes, Danny ripped a line drive. His eyes opened wide as the ball sailed down the left field line. There it was! The game winner! Then his heart dropped as he saw the umpire throw both of his arms toward foul territory. In his head, his dad yelled, "Stop, swinging that damn bat in the house and throw out the empty beer bottles!"

The pitcher pounded his glove, wound up, and fired again. Danny watched the ball rise, high enough above his hands where he was coached never to swing. He moved the bat ever so slightly toward the ball, but stopped his wrists just before the bat crossed the front part of home plate.

"Strike three!" said the umpire, pulling his right arm above his shoulder.

June 23 – 10 p.m.

After the kids and Mary Jo had gone to sleep, Dan hit the Internet to research reincarnation. He needed to know more about old souls coming back to life before he ventured to Gettysburg.

What he found out proved to be more compelling than he had thought. He discovered a man named Jeffrey Keane, a retired firefighter from Westport, Connecticut. Dan sharpened his focus through the rum buzz in his brain to read Keane's story.

> Like most people, I was stumbling through life minding my own business when all at once the world started having its way with me. Suddenly, the ordinary became the extraordinary, and strange occurrences in my life started to make sense. . . . I decided to accept the fact that I was being guided and opened myself up to what life wanted to show me. Long after I had been convinced of a past life, unusual events kept reinforcing my conclusions, so much so that the only reason I could come up with for such revelations was that I was to share them with others.

Dan saw that Keane had never read a book on the Civil War or had any desire to know about that time; yet, while on vacation with his wife, he felt drawn to visit the battlefield at Antietam, Maryland, the site where nearly twenty-four thousand men were killed in the greatest single-day loss of American lives in history.

Once there, a wave of grief, sadness, and anger washed over me. Without warning, I was suddenly consumed by sensations. Burning tears ran down my cheeks. It became difficult to breathe. I gasped for air, as I stood transfixed in the old roadbed.

Keane had another revelation that placed him on that field at Antietam—standing over his own body, which had been shot full of holes. Then, at the bottom of the screen, another detail of this man's experience pushed Dan back in his chair. .Keane had determined he possessed the soul of Colonel John B. Gordon of the Sixth Alabama Regiment.

"What's with this Alabama thing?" Dan let out a nervous laugh.

A comforting thought jumped into his head. There are at least two men who think they possess the souls of Confederate soldiers. Maybe there was an annual convention somewhere in Alabama for an entire reincarnation of Lee's army of Northern Virginia.

June 24 – 8 a.m.

Dan gnawed on a bagel while he watched a colorful flock of songbirds take turns at the backyard feeder. The kids were off to school to the first of their last three days before summer vacation.

After a workout at the gym, Mary Jo would meet a friend for lunch. Her interest in having a day for herself turned out to be good news for Dan. A night's sleep can change a mood. She smiled over her cup of coffee and offered to pick up the kids at the bus stop. The early morning sun advertised a beautiful yet cool summer day.

She was happy to know that he had secured a friend to go along with him to Gettysburg.

"I called Gary Miller at six thirty this morning and asked him to go along," said Dan.

"Was he awake? I'm sure that went over well."

"First, he thought the hospital was calling to tell him his wife's mother had died, and once he we got past that, he told me he had scheduled a full day of yard work, and once we got past that, an offer to pay for his admission and buy him lunch closed the deal."

"You know what I'm praying for," she said.

"Yes, I do. After I find this kid, Fox News will be called to the field to interview me. Then, it's on to the late night talk shows, and you'll come with me to explain how wonderful it is to be married to a sixty-year-old man who has now become a 164-year-old boy."

"Wrong," she said with a wry smile. "I'm praying the neighbors don't find out how silly this story, is or I'll be the woman wearing the paper bag on my head when I pick up the kids at school."

⟋⟋⟍⟍

The drive to Gettysburg with Gary Miller set the tone for Dan to find himself on the battlefield.

"Are you kidding me, Dan?" Gary said. "You don't believe in diddly-squat unless science proves it exists. Now you're looking for a dead soldier from your mind—no, wait a second, now you're looking for YOU at Gettysburg?"

Excellent, thought Dan. That was exactly why he wanted Gary Miller to come with him. Gary believed in reincarnation, but he would never buy anything that Dan was selling.

"I know what you're up to, my friend," Gary said, as he punched Dan in the arm. "You're taking me here to try to convince me that my theories about souls coming back to life are all bullshit."

"We'll have to see about that," said Dan.

"I'll bet you ten bucks you're looking for the last laugh. You might even pretend all this shit is real before you tell me it's some kind of April fool's joke, even though it's June."

"I'll tell you what, Gary. If this story is real, you owe me twenty bucks. If not, I will gladly pay you double at forty."

"You're on, Danny boy, but I have to see undeniable proof that you and this Johnny Reb are the same guy."

∞

Gettysburg National Park opened its doors just as they arrived. A few school buses turned into the parking lot ahead of Dan. He thought about the average teenager and grade school kid coming here. A day away from the classroom and goofing around on the bus would be the highlights for most of them.

Dan sprang for tickets to the Cyclorama. He didn't want to go directly to the battlefield. He'd rather do this venue first and then ease into the main event.

Gary walked around searching for donuts and coffee. He was a smart man, but he played the dumbass role, except when it came to an intellectual argument. He would compete as hard to win a debate as Pete Rose did to win a baseball game. Gary was no Civil War buff. He would avoid engaging in any debate about Gettysburg, and yet, he would never wave the white flag to surrender, no matter what Dan did to win the bet.

The recorded narrator started to describe the three-day encounter while Dan and Gary, along with some noisy schoolchildren, stood before the revolving depictions of the battle. The guns began to fire through speakers in the ceiling along with simulated cannon explosions. Almost immediately, Dan's right ear began to throb.

Okay, so loud noises have always bothered me. No big deal. No connection.

After the presentation, which Gary called "cool," they moved along to the museum. Dan examined artifacts: drinking cups, guns, and ammunition. The pieces seemed familiar to him, but at the same time, those thoughts might be nothing more than his will wanting to prove an association or a trick his mind was playing.

He searched through photographs looking to match a face imprinted in his brain with that of Joshua Park's. Nothing there. Dan assumed the kid must have been a private or a PFC. Most of the photographs were those of officers.

"You ready for the field?" asked Gary. "So far the only gray uniform I've ever seen you wear was Mike Piazza's Mets jersey when we went to a Phillies game last summer."

Dan decided not to address that remark. He just nodded to Gary who led the way out of the museum.

June 24 – 1:30 p.m.

They stood looking upon the field that had burdened Robert E. Lee with more than seven thousand Confederate casualties on that third of July afternoon. Dan stared out toward the copse of trees, what history has called the high-water mark of the Confederacy—the farthest point to the north that the South advanced during the five-year war.

A guide leading a group of grade-school students disturbed Dan's attention. While the kids were being told about battle strategies, some of them goofed around, laughing and pushing each other. Their teacher tried to restore order, but her frustration was obvious. "You better pay attention!" she shouted. "There will be a quiz tomorrow!"

Dan marveled at how this would be his second search for a spiritual epiphany in the midst of a public place. Digging into his soul with Lotz had played out within the chatter of office workers in the hall. Now he would attempt to discover if he had died on this battlefield while school kids were pinching each other's rear ends.

Gary stopped to talk to the teacher. He would talk to a tree if he thought it would listen. The swagger of her backside must have sparked his attention, enough of a reason for him to pursue a conversation.

Meanwhile, Dan stepped onto the edge of the field as if it was covered by thin ice, afraid he might sink into an abyss of yesteryear. He peered across the landscape, thinking how bucolic this present scene would be for a watercolor painting to hang over the fireplace. He took a small step forward, then another step, and then one more. The air was still. The sun blazed down upon his face, sending a rush of heat through his body. He walked forward about ten more feet and stopped. An orange monarch butterfly danced across the low-lying brush in front of him.

A swift breeze swept away the stillness, cooling off the sun's burn from his face.

He dared to step farther.

At the next moment, the breeze stopped. An invisible weight dropped into his chest. In his mind's eye, a black cloud had eclipsed the sun. Distant sounds of screams and groans funneled into ears. He took one step back from what danger he feared lay ahead upon the field.

"Hey, buddy, you can't walk out there."

The voice startled Dan back into reality. He turned to see a man in a park security uniform waving his arms. Standing alongside was Gary. "You cannot walk on the field," the ranger repeated.

Dan hurried back. "Sorry, I didn't realize how far out I had gone."

"No problem. It happens more often than you might think," the ranger said with a grin. "I'm sure you can understand. We believe this is consecrated ground here, for obvious reasons."

"Oh, I completely agree," Dan said. "We lost so many men here, most in the prime of their lives."

"Yes, sir. There were soldiers as young as twelve years and as old as eighty that fought and died here."

"What a damn shame."

"Well, you enjoy the rest of your visit, sir, and if you have any questions, you can track down one of our tour guides. They'll be wearing identification badges."

"Thank you," said Dan, removing his Mets cap to wipe the sweat from his forehead.

The ranger departed in his golf cart. Dan looked at Gary. "Why didn't you warn me he was coming?"

"I was talking with the teacher. I wasn't paying attention to where you were."

"Shocker," said Dan, as he gazed up the field. "Let's drive to the top of the hill."

∞

The copse of trees stood in a cluster, forming a huge umbrella that shaded visitors from the hot sun. Once more, Dan admired how pastoral the field appeared from the hill, when back on that day, there had been so much carnage that the blood that spilled onto the ground must have painted a deep red over the brilliant gold.

He sensed the futility of those Rebel soldiers who somehow managed to get this far only to be shot down or captured by the Union army. It's like hitting that blast to the top of the fence only to have the outfielder snatch from over the wall the game-winning homerun.

Now, with the field burned to gold again by a forgiving sun, the living landscape appeared to have forgotten that this field had been an arena of war. The stain of death had been washed away by years of rain and replaced by new growth and new life. Dan first thought that Mother Nature seemed to have lost her compassion for the men from both sides who had died here. She should hang a permanent black cloud over the field to keep the mourning fires burning. Then again, he reconsidered; although the soul can be scarred forever, the serenity of the field at modern-day Gettysburg eased the pain of history's brutality, so that humanity could move forward from its past.

Gary followed Dan to the monument where General Armistead, carrying the torch for his cause, reportedly fell wounded. Dan touched the stone, its cool surface resisting the midday sun. He stepped below to the wall where Union soldiers had waited until they were able to see the Confederates entering through a curtain of black smoke. Once given the order, they fired at will at targets no more than twenty feet away.

Dan thought he heard a faint voice calling to him from the other side of the wall. His heart thumped against his chest. He stepped over a layer of stones and walked forward before he suddenly stopped. With his brain spinning out images of the battle like a movie projector, he freeze-framed a grizzled soldier lying on the ground behind him, bleeding and cursing.

"*Them Yankee devil bastards won't never get me!*"

Carter!

Dan turned his attention to the right. Another soldier shot down appeared to be dead, yet he lay on the ground with his eyes locked open toward the sky.

Waterson!

When he turned around, Dan's ears rang so loud that he heard nothing, except the dulled vibrations of gunfire. He grabbed the sides of his head, closed his eyes, lost his balance, and fell to his knees. Opening his eyes again, he stood again and saw that he had fallen in front of another dead soldier, one with a very familiar face, that of a friend. Words spoke from dead man's lips.

"*See you on the other side.*"

Jenkins!

An arrow of disgust struck in the center of Dan's chest. He released a river of rage from the damn in his eyes.

A swirling gust of wind surrounded his body again. All his tension and tears lifted into the air. He closed his eyes, breathing inside a circle of peace. He opened them again. The outline of a young girl standing below the copse of trees appeared before him.

"*Joshua! Joshua Park!*"

Dan opened his mouth to call to Becky, but she vanished along with the breeze. Instead, he saw with rifle raised a soldier in blue.

"No! No! Don't shoot!" shouted Dan.

A voice shouted from the top of the hill. "*Parky! Parky! It's Becky. I'm here, Parky!*"

Dan fell to his knees again. His baseball cap fell from his head.

"*Come to me, Parky. You come home to me right now, Joshua Park. Do you hear?*"

Dan stood up, his eyes filled with new tears. He looked ahead. The man in blue still pointed his rifle at him. Dan dropped to the ground, running his fingers through the short grass, feeling for his gun, finding nothing. He stood up, and with his right hand, he squeezed an imaginary piece of paper.

"Becky? Becky, where are you? I can't see you, Becky." Dan turned around and around, spinning his body until he became so dizzy he lost all sense of direction. "I want to go with you, Becky. Let's go home!"

Somehow, he stopped spinning and stood frozen before the man in blue. A white flash from the barrel of the soldier's gun shook the ground he stood upon. Dan grabbed his chest. He staggered two steps forward, then one backward, but managed to stay on his feet.

"Parky? Where are you? Please come back to me!"

"Dan. Dan?"

"Sir, you'll have to come with me now."

Dan caught his breath. He looked down at his arm. The park ranger had a grip on it.

"Dan? You okay? It's Gary. Gary. Remember me?"

Still trembling, Dan had no power to move. Gary and the ranger pulled him off the field, his legs dragging upon the ground as if he were a giant rag doll. Regaining a sense of reality, he placed his hands on the hood of the ranger's Jeep to steady himself. People had gathered around. Dan looked up to see several school kids laughing and pointing to him. Next to the Jeep, he heard a man speak to a woman who stood by. "He's probably hallucinating the battle," said the man. "I bet they got nut jobs like him running all over this place more than you think."

"Are you okay, sir?"

The ranger placed his hand upon Dan's shoulder. He looked down at the man's badge. The sun's reflection off the silver medal burned his eyes. Dan opened his mouth, but no words came out. Then, releasing an energy that had been trapped inside him for much too long, he spoke from his conscience rather than his will.

"Joshua. Call me Joshua, Joshua Park. And Becky. She's my girlfriend. She wanted me to come home with her. I-I didn't, though."

Dan lifted his right hand to find something he thought would be there. He bent down to search the ground. "Where's the letter?" he demanded. "It was from Becky. Where did it go? I must have dropped it on the field. I have to go back and get it."

Gary and the ranger held Dan back. They turned him around and, after some resistance, pushed him into the Jeep. As the vehicle moved away, Dan stared out the window at the battlefield..

How many times do I have to die here?

June 24 – 3 p.m.

While an EMT checked his vitals in the park's first aid center, Dan wondered if he ought to be ashamed of himself. His anger kicked out any chance of that.

Gary was slumped into a chair on the other side of the room. A man wearing a brown suit came in and sat down across the table from Dan and waved for the EMT to leave.

"Mr. Bryant, I'm Bill Harper, park administrator. I'm told you appear to be physically fine, but would you care to tell me what you think happened out on that battlefield today?"

Dan realized he had to put up a front to get out of this predicament, even though one side of his brain had a different story to tell. He wanted to speak for Joshua Park, whose voice had been silenced by a bullet to his chest, but he had to maintain control. He didn't need any more problems added to his growing list.

Dan's angry voice spoke to his mind, but he stopped the words before they could escape from his lips. *Didn't I tell you? I was shot dead after all my boys were murdered by those Yankee bastards. I lost everyone that mattered to me, especially my Becky. I will never see her again. Put that story in your damn museum, you idiot!*

"I guess I had a bit of a breakdown," Dan answered aloud. "There's been a lot of stress in my life lately. I am truly sorry I brought all that here today."

Harper placed his hands on the table. "Do you feel that you participated in the battle, Mr. Bryant?"

What did I just tell you? I'm nineteen years old, scared out of my fucking mind, tripping over severed arms and stepping on blown-out eyeballs, and you bring in busloads of ignorant kids who are going to leave here with shopping bags full of paper flags and toy soldiers and plastic Civil War medals from your shit-filled souvenir store. And I'll never even know where the hell they threw my rotting corpse!

"No. No. It's nothing like that at all," said Dan. "I feel awful. I forgot where I was when I put on that spectacle, but I'm fine now. Really, I'm good."

Harper's grin said bullshit. "If it's any comfort, you're not the first visitor to react as if you participated personally in the Battle of Gettysburg," he said. "It's not an everyday occurrence, but in my time here, we've had a few people who have believed they were reincarnations of Confederate or Union soldiers and have had emotional meltdowns on the field."

"So, what's *your* take on reincarnation?" Dan asked, fighting harder against the angry voice in his head.

"I have no reasons to believe. The burden of proof would be on the person who thinks he's an old soul returned to life, and I have yet to see undeniable evidence."

So I have to find my trashed cadaver somewhere around here and do a DNA test to give you my burden of proof? Or how about I find you the letter from Becky I was holding in my hand 140 fucking years ago! Or maybe you should add a room onto your museum where whackos like me can tell your visitors real-life Civil War horror stories and then autograph their fucking ticket stubs. Better yet, we can have a North vs. South wrestling tournament. I get in the ring wearing my soldier grays and wrestle some other nut job in Union blue who thinks he's General Winfield S. fucking Hancock!

Harper stood up to leave, and Dan took the cue to stand as well.

"My advice to you, Mr. Bryant, is that you should see a psychiatrist about your disorder so this doesn't happen again in a public place."

That's it, thought Dan. He could not hold back any longer. "A good idea, Mr. Harper," said Dan. "And if he tells me that I have to face my fears to eliminate them, then I might just have to return to this battlefield." Dan glared across the table at Harper, who was still wearing that bullshit smile.

"Next time, Mr. Harper, I will come in full uniform representing the Confederate States of America. And I will be carrying a Sharps rifle with me. I will let you know in advance of my arrival. You might want to charge extra admission on that day because your visitors are going to see one hell of a show."

Dan placed his hands down on the table and leaned forward.

"And this time, Mr. Harper, the Army of Northern Virginia is going to *win!*"

∞

Halfway through the drive back, Gary broke the silence between them. "You're either crazy, or you need twenty bucks real bad, or you really were or are that Joshua whatever the hell his name was—or is."

Dan slammed down the gas pedal. "I need the twenty bucks."

June 24 – 7:30 p.m.

When Dan opened the door from the garage to enter the house, there stood Mary Jo in the hallway. The look on her face said that she was not about to speak the words, "Welcome home, honey."

"What the hell happened to you there?" she barked

"How did you find out?"

"Gary called Shelia while you were being taken to the first aid station, and she called to warn me."

"Some friend he is. I knew I should have gone with someone else."

"Dan, you need to see someone about this. I'm worried, and so are the kids. Jacob overheard me on the phone, and he started to get angry. He thinks you might flip out at his baseball game this weekend. Then Katy got scared. She's been crying, too."

"You're right. Tomorrow I'm checking myself into a nuthouse. I'll be in the dead soldier wing, whistling "Dixie" right next to my man Robert E. Lee. He and I will be planning our next attack on Gettysburg."

"Cut the crap, Dan. You're delusional. You need a psychiatrist. I got enough to handle with the kids and this house. Now I find out my sixty-year-old husband is playing war and making a fool of himself."

He attacked her with her own voice, hoping to fend off any further incoming missiles. "Well, now! After I get released from the loony bin, I'll just scoot on down to the Happy fucking Meadows old folks home and see if they have any openings. If I get in, then maybe you can have the kids send a card every now and then. I'd like ones with pictures of oak trees, if you don't mind."

"You have an appointment at two o'clock on Thursday with Dr. Lowery in Allentown."

"Oh, good. Gives me some time to go out and buy me a Confederate uniform. Want to look the part for the doc, you know. Probably not a good idea to bring along a Rebel rifle. Might not get past the receptionist. What do you think?"

Mary Jo picked up a vase from the counter and flung it at Dan, barely missing his head before it smashed against the wall behind him. "I think I've had enough of you!" she cried. "I have better things to do than get insulted by a man, excuse me, by a *child* who has lost his mind. You need to get a grip, Dan! You're a mess!"

"So you've had enough of this old wackadooley, huh? Maybe I should just limp out into the woods like an old dog and die alone!"

"*Old* is the right word, Dan. It's bad enough that you're my father's age, but now you think you're some, some, *corpse* that you didn't even know existed before last week!"

Mary Jo had already left the hall, but Dan knew there was more coming.

"I can't do this anymore!" he heard her cry. "I am tired of being a prisoner of your stupid mind. I want my own life!"

She slammed the bedroom door, a sound that frightened Dan more than a barrage of artillery from the Union army.

After the bullet he took on the battlefield and the slam of the door by the only woman he had ever loved, Dan came to a somber realization.

This was the second time he had died on the same day.

June 25 – After the Midnight Hour

A sleepless night fueled by too many Bacardi and Cokes left Dan fighting a revolution in his mind. He grabbed his baseball cap and a broom handle and stumbled out the front door into the dark of midnight, dimly lit by a misty moon. *Perfect*, he thought. As he staggered left and right up the road, he invited Joshua Park to jump out of his soul and into his head.

"So, my friend," said Dan aloud, "you gonna walk up this street with me looking for bluebellies, or do I have to go it alone?"

An animal of some kind ran across the street about ten yards ahead.

"Bang, bang, you're dead." Dan pulled back the bolt from his broom-handle, make-believe rifle.

He laughed so loud a woman walking her dog up the street stopped and turned around. "It's me!" Dan yelled. "Mr. Joshua Park, private first class of the Alabama Thirteenth." He was aware now that he was speaking in Southern drawl. "I'm gonna fight my way up this damn road cuz my little honey, Becky, she's at the top. She been waitin' for me for well over a hunnert years!" He laughed again, this time with a tinge of evil in his alcoholic voice. "Now she's what ya call one patient lady waitin' that long for her man, don't ya think!"

The woman turned away. Dan saw her and the dog jog off into the distant black. "You better run, you bluebelly sumbitch!" he shouted after her.

Dan heard something rustle in the woods off to the side of the road. He took off after the noise like a wild horse romping through the brush. A thornbush ripped across his right cheek. He wiped warm blood onto the back of his hand. "Bastards! You want a piece of me that bad? Well, not if I get you first, and this time I aim to kill!"

He fired his fake gun again, blasting the woods with a shot, reload, shot, reload, shot, until thoroughly spent, he stumbled into a pit of weeds and bushes. He dropped the broomstick, covered his face with his hands, and rolled over onto his back. With his head upon a flat rock, he fell fast asleep.

Dan awakened to the tingle of an insect crawling across his face. He staggered to his feet, his face numbed by the rock his head had used as a pillow. A pain in his chest shot down both his arms and reminded him that he no longer was a young Joshua Park. He was an old Dan Bryant. He groaned loud enough to chase away a nearby squirrel that had stopped nearby to stare him down.

Ambling down the street toward his house, Dan squinted at the morning sunrise slivering through a gray cloud left from the last wisp of the night sky. The emerging light brought his attention back to his argument with Mary Jo.

Jacob was angry. Katy had cried. His wife had called him a child, subtracting his manhood, reducing his epiphany at Gettysburg to an act of public foolishness.

A blast of wind swept away his hatred of the world. He promised to shut Joshua Park inside a sealed box he would store somewhere in his brain and be the husband Mary Jo deserved and the father Jacob and Katy loved.

Dan approached the driveway. A sudden cloudburst poured a bucket of summer rain upon him. He stopped, lifting his head to the sky, letting the cool water wash his face. The rain felt good, purging him of everything that had gripped his mind. Mother Nature's baptism welcomed him to a new day and a return to himself. With blood running though his veins like an uncorked spring, a reborn Dan Bryant jumped up the stairs and into his house.

He tiptoed through the front door. Mary Jo would be in the kitchen as usual. With his conviction to not allow her to interrupt his redemption speech, he wiped the rain from his face and began to speak from the foyer.

"Johnny Reb is dead, Mary Jo. Joshua Park is done for good. I'm not chasing his ghost anymore. There's nothing to gain. You were right." He raised his voice to make sure she could hear it all. "Everything has been about me. I've been selfish, not giving you a chance to become the person you want to be. It stops now. I want to be your husband again, the man you love, and the father our children deserve.

"I am ready to support everything you want to do. I love you, Mary Jo," he said through a crack in his voice. "I have never stopped loving you, and I'm going to prove it to you all over again. I will not lose you. What matters to me is here, in our home, what I have right in front of me."

There. He had said it, but instead of her voice, a dead silence from the kitchen filled his ears. The kids should have been eating breakfast. Mary Jo should have been at her customary place behind the stove, frying up some eggs.

Dan walked slowly into the kitchen.

He found no one.

He saw no plates, no silverware, no napkins. There was a single piece of white paper at his place at the table. He picked it up and saw Mary Jo's handwriting before he began to read a single word.

> Dan,
>
> I didn't sleep all night. Katy crawled in bed with me, and Jacob checked on us almost every hour.
>
> I'm a mess. Katy cries and misses you. Jacob is angry.
>
> We can't do this anymore. You need professional help.
>
> I took the kids to my mother's. From there I will take them to school and pick them up.
>
> I need time. I'm disappointed in you. Please do not contact me when you read this letter. I'm

in no mood to hear anything from you right now.
I will have the kids call you after dinner.

I am not coming home. I need to figure out
my life.

Mary Jo

While reading the last sentence, Dan's hand began to shake.
He walked to the counter where the near-empty Bacardi rum
bottle remained from last night.

He opened the back door, and with one swing of his arm, he
fired the bottle right down the middle of the trunk of a pin oak
tree. The sound of glass shattering and the rum dripping from
the bark soothed him for a second until he realized what had just
happened was not imagined by his already overburdened mind.

Desperate thoughts raced through his head. Call and apologize. Show up with flowers and balloons. He fought back the
tears for now, but why not go to them in a full-blown meltdown
so they could see how much he loved them?

Okay, he said to himself. *Let's figure this out to avoid any
confrontation that would only make matters worse.*

He decided to write a detailed plan, a plan that must work.
He would buy a bottle of good champagne to go with king crab
legs, Mary Jo's favorite, and get some steaks for him and the
kids for tomorrow tonight.

Yes, tomorrow night!

Why not? The kids would miss him and would want to come
home.

Be creative. Be honest. Maybe try to get Mary Jo to laugh
about all this. Loosen things up.

Never mind, said the other side of his brain. *She will never
laugh about this.*

He sat down and wrote more notes. No matter what it would
take, Dan would have his family back in twenty-four hours.

Something hit his mind after that thought. Mary Jo couldn't
find out about the three hundred dollars he had just spent.

The UPS man had delivered an authentic flag of the Confederacy to the house that afternoon.

Just after sunset, Dan snuck up on his mother-in-law's front lawn. First, he leaned their largest wedding picture against a tree. Then, he propped up a framed family Christmas photo. Next, he erected a super-sized copy of his appointment with the psychiatrist in Allentown.

Now for the grand finale, the clincher to bring them back home.

His friend had created two life-sized cardboard stand-ups in his sign shop. Dan stood up a Confederate soldier. Next to him, he put up a same sized figure of himself appearing to be swinging a bat toward the soldier's head. Behind the cardboard figures, he placed a battery-powered boom box on the lawn.

Dan drove away to the fading sounds of Trace Atkins singing "Every Light in the House Is On." He would go home, light up the house like a Christmas tree, and wait for his family to return.

June 16 – 6 p.m.

Dan kept the champagne chilled and the crab legs and steaks on ice. He flipped every light switch on in the house. Three days later, with the house still ablaze and the food still in the freezer, Dan was having his scheduled talk with the kids. Katy cried about how much she missed him. Jacob gave one-word answers to his questions about school and Jessie.

Mary Jo ignored his requests to take the phone. His texts to her went unanswered.

On the fourth night, with all the lights burning bright, Dan sat alone at the kitchen table, eating a peanut-butter-and-jelly sandwich for dinner.

He heard a car stopping in the driveway. When he opened the front door, Jacob and Katy bounded up the steps into his welcoming arms. Then they raced upstairs to their rooms, leaving Mary Jo at the door holding her suitcase.

Dan opened his mouth to speak.

"You don't have to say you're sorry," she said. "That menagerie you planted on my mother's lawn took care of that."

Dan opened his mouth to speak again.

"I had a long talk with my mom," she said. "Actually, she had a long talk with me. She was able to get me to see what you are going through and that you and I have to try to figure this out for the sake of the kids and for the sake of our marriage."

Mary Jo took a step into the foyer and put down her luggage.

"But that's not why I came back." She took a deep breath, and Dan heard a hitch in her throat. "I don't know if I was dreaming or what, or maybe you willed him into me, but in the middle of last night, I saw him." She took another breath and looked up to the ceiling and then back at Dan. "I saw Joshua. I clearly saw the same face you described. He looked so . . . so young and handsome and . . . well, I felt sorry for him. He never had the chance to live his life, to have a family. It was weird, Dan. This vision, or dream, whatever it was, pulled me right into your story. What I'm trying to say is that there's no doubt that I'm part of this thing now.

"So I'm enlisting in your battalion for saving Private Park," she said. "I cancelled your appointment with the psychiatrist because I thought if you're going crazy, then so am I." She took a deep breath. "We'll go together to the nuthouse."

He opened his mouth to speak once again, but he found no words to say.

Mary Jo turned toward the stairs. "Oh, I do ask one favor of you. Please don't fly that Confederate flag in the yard. It wouldn't be in our best interests to have a reincarnation of the entire Union Army marching up our driveway."

∞

Dan grilled the porterhouses and steamed the crab legs. He and Mary Jo sipped champagne; the kids laughed through dinner, except for Jacob, of course, when the discussion turned to fantasy wedding plans for Jessie and him. Katy suggested they get married at Cinderella's Castle in Disney World. Dan said Jessie's dad had already booked the church hall for a date ten years from now.

"The backyard would be fine for the reception," chimed Mary Jo, as she finished her second glass of champagne. "As long as Jacob picks up the dog poop. I'd hate to see Jessie's gown get dragged through that."

Jacob stepped away from the knockdown pitches better this time. He did not retaliate, especially since he was about to play soccer with Jessie just before sunset.

When the kids excused themselves from the table, Dan shifted the subject.

"So how was your class?" he blurted through a swallow of champagne.

"Well, now that you've asked, one thing I learned was that the greatest single consequence to our health is stress."

Here she goes again, he thought. This time he would bite his tongue and listen.

"I do worry about your health," she said.

Dan relaxed. "I've dumped enough crap on us both to fill up Citi Field," he said.

"First of all," she replied, "You can't give up chasing Joshua Park. You need to find some kind of final answer or explanation, even if it's proof that the whole damn story is a fabrication of your mind—and now of my mind, too."

"What about us?" Dan asked.

"To be honest, how can there be an us until this ghost proves why he chose you?"

"What about you? I mean, what about pursuing your dream?"

"Dan, I will never stop loving you, but I need to have my own life too. I need to be me. It doesn't matter if you support what I want to do or not. I am going to complete my studies and start my own wellness business."

"I *will* support you," he said, "and that's a promise."

"Well, then, do me a favor and talk to Joshua about that. Three's a crowd. Maybe he can loosen his grip on your brain once in a while, so you can give me some ideas for my new website."

∞

The summer night's song of the katydids filtered through the windows. With the kids asleep and the bottle of champagne emptied, an air of expectation filled the master bedroom. *Love need not be the center of physical intimacy*, thought Dan. He wanted his touch upon Mary Jo's body to release any worries that were still locked inside her mind.

She blossomed for him like a beautiful orchid. Anointed by the delicate scent of almond oil, she aroused his senses to the very edge of his losing control. Sensual foreplay became physical poetry until their heartbeats calmed and the night's sleep promised an early morning encore before the start of a new day.

June 26 – 9 a.m.

The talk at the breakfast table on Saturday refreshed the tradition of a family adventure day. Throw everyone in the car. Drive anywhere with no destination planned. Follow the road to discovery.

With excitement abounding from Katy and a whine of resistance from Jacob, Dan turned their SUV onto Route 93 toward the city of Hazleton. About three quarters of the way there, he saw a sign for Eckley Miners' Village.

"What's that?" asked Mary Jo.

"I remember reading something about it," said Dan. "It's an old coalmining town preserved from the late nineteenth century. I think there's a museum, too."

"Sounds pretty interesting. Let's check it out."

Groans expelled from the back seat were ignored. As they entered the parking lot, Mary Jo pointed to a sign: "Civil War Reenactment Today."

"Mary Jo, I had no idea," Dan pleaded. "You have to believe me. Let's turn around and keep going."

"It's okay. Really, it's okay. Let's go see." She leaned over and kissed Dan on his cheek. After he parked the car, Mary Jo put her hand on his shoulder. "You might want to ask if they have an extra uniform lying around. Our kids would get a kick out of watching their father play war with grown men who shoot guns that go bang-bang."

Dan studied her face. She chuckled once; then, she broke into a loud laugh he had not heard from her in months. This time Mary Jo wasn't playing head games against him. She made it clear that she wanted to be his teammate.

"Maybe they'll let me hang out with the Confederates," he said. "I'll offer to lead the troops in a rendition of 'Them Old Cotton Fields Back Home.'" Dan placed both of his hands on Mary Jo's face. He kissed her mouth so hard she pushed him back.

"It's good to know I can still take your breath away," he joked.

She squeezed his hand, and he understood. He paraded his family to the ticket office with his head held high, realizing that all was right in the Bryant universe again.

They arrived at the battlefield just in time for the main event.

This was not to be a re-creation of a mega fight like Gettysburg. Dan counted six Confederates and a dozen Yanks. He figured it must be difficult for some of the reenactors to get away from the wives and kids.

The skirmish started with the grays setting up two clusters of three men behind large rocks and fallen timber. The blues lined up in straight military march. On command, they marched forward until they approached a clearing in a field where the grays opened fire, picking off a Yank here and there.

Dan watched with little intent, but through the corner of his eye, he could see Mary Jo sneaking looks of concern at him.

The blues marched onward. Dan covered his ears with his hands. About forty yards away, the command was given to commence firing, resulting in a volley of shots that knocked down a few more men from both sides. By an easy count, Dan could see the Yanks were left with two men standing, while three Rebels fired guns back at their enemy. The skirmish ended with the Union army waving a white surrender flag. With approving applause from the crowd, both sides extended their hands in a symbol of peace.

At the back of the crowd, an Abraham Lincoln character began to recite the Gettysburg Address. With everyone's attention turned toward Lincoln, Dan watched the Confederate reenactors, in two lines of three, step toward him in formal military march.

As they passed, the soldier in the middle of the back row, appearing to be the youngest in the group, suddenly turned his head and tipped his cap to Dan.

"Mary Jo, did you see that?" he asked.

"See what? I was watching Lincoln."

"One of the Confederates broke protocol and tipped his cap to me."

"Maybe he was showing appreciation for you being here."

"Could be," Dan said, "but there might be another meaning in that gesture."

"Dan, it's just a reenactment. He can't see you as Joshua Park."

"Would you mind if I . . . ?"

She placed her hand on her hip.

Dan smacked a kiss on her cheek and ran down the path toward the departing soldiers. He moved through the crowded main dirt road with no sight of the troops. About a hundred yards away, he looked to his left. He saw a man dressed in gray, breaking down camp.

"Excuse me. My name is Dan Bryant," he said.

"Hello. I'm Ross Tucker."

"I'm looking for a young man from your troop. He was in the middle of the back row when you left the field."

"You mean Toby—Toby Waterson. He had to leave in a hurry. Got a pregnant wife back home down South that he needs to check on."

"Waterson, you say? Where's he staying?"

"He's up the road in Beaver Meadows. Not sure of the address, but you can find him at the Grace Baptist Church in Hazleton tomorrow morning at the ten o'clock service."

Game on again, thought Dan. He had a gut feeling that this kid knew something that might help him find out more about Joshua Park.

Dan waited in the parking lot of Grace Baptist Church until most of the congregation had departed. Uncertain if he could recognize the young man's face again, he stopped a white-haired woman as she was getting into her car. "Good morning, ma'am. Would you know where I might find Toby Waterson?"

"Who wants to know?" she said with a curious pitch in her voice.

"My name is Dan Bryant," trying not to sound too suspicious. "I saw him yesterday at Eckley Miners' Village, and I think I know him from somewhere."

That didn't sound too convincing, he thought. She studied his face for a moment. "He's usually the last one out. You can find him in the vestibule."

"Thank you, ma'am. You have yourself a great day."

Dan bounded up the stairs, nodding his head to people passing by. Once inside, he walked up the center aisle of the church and saw an open door to the side of the altar that led to a small room. He walked in. There stood the soldier he'd seen on the battlefield, this time dressed in a green sports shirt and casual black pants. He had waves of brown hair that crossed over his forehead and looked to be in his twenties.

"Can I help you, sir?" he asked.

"My name is Dan Bryant. I saw you reenact at the village yesterday, and you nodded to me."

The young man arched an eyebrow. "You certainly take a simple nod most serious by coming all the way here to find me today." He extended his hand, and Dan complied with a shake. "I'm Toby Waterson. Come sit down with me out front."

They took seats in the first pew in front of a white marble sculpture of the resurrected Jesus. As the late morning sun filtered through the stained-glass windows, thin white lines of light streamed upon the beatific face of Christ. Dan wondered if God had arrived to witness their meeting. Just in case, he would mind his manners and say nothing to elicit confrontation. And not knowing if Baptists believed in reincarnation, he decided that wouldn't be a question to ask.

"Isn't he beautiful?" asked Toby, pointing up at the sculpture.

"Absolutely splendid," answered Dan.

They made small talk about the weather and the area. Dan was quite impressed with the way the young man presented himself. After a pause in their chat, Dan's impatience forced him to redirect their conversation.

"Why did you break protocol and nod to me yesterday?"

"I sensed a familiarity." Toby sat back in the pew. "I believe I know you from somewhere. Were you ever in Clay County, Alabama?"

"No, never. Why would you put me there?"

"That's my neck of the woods," said Toby. "I'm staying in Beaver Meadows with my in-laws for a few weeks while my wife is home, preparing to have our first baby. Her folks are up in age. Her dad had a stroke, so I offered to help them settle into an assisted living complex." Toby explained that he'd met his wife, Clarissa, a few years ago when he had come north for a reenactment at Gettysburg. They fell in love and moved back to Clay County, where he was born and raised.

"What got you interested in doing Civil War reenactments?" asked Dan, trying to solve the mystery of how Toby might know him.

"In my neighborhood, we call it the War of Northern Aggression," he said. "I have ancestors who fought in the war, all the way from Chickamauga to Gettysburg. Don't have all the facts, but many, I believe, died in battle."

Dan's curiosity about this young man was piqued further.

"Mr. Bryant, I'm studying to become a minister of this faith—a calling from God, if you will. I reckon he puts people in front of me for a reason. When I saw you yesterday, I had this feeling that you weren't just there as a spectator. When I left the field, I let the thought go, but now here you are, wanting to know what brought you here to me."

"I'm going to fall just short of saying that we knew each other in a previous lifetime," said Dan, "but if that were true and if your finding me has significance, then I'm still left wondering why."

Toby's eyes darted to the sculpture again. The sun had shifted, spreading a soft glow over the head of Jesus.

"Mr. Bryant, were you close with your father?" Toby asked.

"Not at all. Why do you ask?"

"I'm trusting an intuition for a connection between us," he said. "For me, my family genealogy reveals a striking commonality. From as far back as before the war, Waterson men have been absent father figures for every reason from family desertion to sickness that ended in early death and, of course, some as causalities of war." He leaned forward toward the sculpture. "My own father died when I was two years old, and for the longest time I hated a man I had never known."

Dan felt a rush of energy, as if someone had plugged him into an electrical outlet. His body actually jumped, and Toby noticed. "Are you okay, sir?"

"Yes, yes. Just getting a little excited about what you just said because it's sort of my story, too—about the father thing."

"You hated your father, too?"

"Absolutely. Never there emotionally for me. No good memories."

"Have you moved on?"

"Of course, except for the hatred part."

"Well then, you haven't moved on. To do that, Mr. Bryant, I believe you have to make your peace with him."

"Make my peace?"

"A Waterson was killed in the War of Northern Aggression, and since then, every Waterson man has been troubled by psychological disturbances." He turned his head toward Dan. "You might know that my great-great-granddaddy was a man of the Lord." He looked directly into Dan's eyes. "He died at Gettysburg."

"I'm not sure I understand what you're getting at."

"He didn't believe in killing, and yet he sacrificed his life for his people, as Jesus did to give us eternal life. Both carried their crosses so others might live in peace." Dan noticed a hint of anger in Toby's voice. "The devil, Mr. Bryant, doesn't always come in red with horns on his head. He can wear blue." He grinned at Dan. "You sir, may live in the North, but I have a notion you carry a kindred with my people."

"I'm searching for an understanding," said Dan. "I hope you can help me."

"My wife is pregnant with our first child, Mr. Bryant. This gift from God has brought me to a point of understanding my own father. I never realized how hating him was putting the blame in the wrong place. It began back at Gettysburg, where my ancestral grandfather's life ended while he was trying to set an example for how people should live together, the way that Jesus intended."

Dan's eyes narrowed. He made a fist with his right hand. Toby took notice.

"Excuse me, Mr. Bryant, but talking about fathers always gets me kind of worked up. I blamed my father when I should have blamed the mental illness that never allowed him the chance to love me. Do you have children?"

"Jacob is almost fifteen, and Katy is going to be eight." Dan stood up and turned around to face Toby, who stayed seated.

"Mr. Bryant," said Toby, looking up at Dan. "The Lord only asks us to question the meaning of our lives. Our purpose is to find that meaning."

Dan turned to face the sculpture. "If I may change the subject," he said, "how is it that you're going to become a minister and you participate in warfare, even if only in reproduction?"

"War is man's choice to solve problems, not God's. However, I believe that faith in the Lord is an absolute on the field of battle because what else can sustain the sanity of soldiers, their love for their families, and the courage to stare into the face of death that sits at the end of a rifle?"

Dan tried to remember where he had heard that before.

Toby peered at a ceiling mural of Jesus standing at the edge of a mountain. "A Waterson man of God took his final breath at Gettysburg. His body never came home. The Lord lifted him up after he fell to the devil's deed. Now he rests somewhere upon a mountain of peace. His spirit lives on, Mr. Bryant. I carry his soul within me."

"Do you hold any anger about what happened in the war?" Dan asked.

"Mr. Bryant, if I walked into your house today and told you your life was over as you know it, what would you say? Then, what if I told you to live under my laws now, that your ancestors, who gave you the gift of your life and the manner in which you choose to live, have died with their legacies holding no significance at all?"

"Just for the sake of argument," Dan said, having secured enough of a comfort level with Toby, "the history books up here say we punished the South because of slavery. What's your take on that?"

Toby's eyes lifted to Jesus. "Mr. Bryant, sir, this city of Hazleton has a terrible problem with street drugs enslaving the minds of many young people who because of the needle have no promised future. I do not see the government coming here to free these children from the slavery of addiction."

"I'm not quite sure I understand," said Dan.

"In time, society rights its wrongs. The acceptance of homosexuality and inter-racial marriage prove how we evolve. Drugs, like cigarettes, will eventually be eradicated. In God's time, laws would have freed the black man, without the need to murder my ancestral grandfather and so many others on both sides. My granddaddy died at Gettysburg with his gun in one hand, his Bible in the other, and love for all people in his heart, both black and white."

The complexity of this young man fascinated Dan.

"You knew him, Mr. Bryant. I could tell when I saw you yesterday. You were next to my granddaddy at Gettysburg when he was killed. In fact, you were the last person to see him alive."

Dan's jaw dropped. "How do you know this?"

"The curse of what you have seen in your visions I have in my soul, too."

"Why do you call it a curse?" Dan asked.

"A Waterson perished at Gettysburg. His son never forgave the Yanks because he grew up without a father. One night, my granddaddy's boy drank a bottle of whiskey and shot himself in the face. Some years later, *his* son was stabbed to death in a New York barroom just because he refused to remove his jacket that had an emblem of a Confederate battle flag sewn onto the sleeve.

"I have my demons too, Mr. Bryant. I pray every day for God to spare me from avenging my ancestors, and yet I believe the Lord has sent every Waterson into this world to fight and defeat the devil himself."

"So how do you move forward?" asked Dan.

"Time will tell." Toby took a deep breath. "Time *must* tell."

After exchanging cell phone numbers, Dan picked himself up to leave. Toby grabbed his arm. "We're still fighting our way up that damn hill, Joshua, fighting to free ourselves from what keeps our souls locked in chains. Keep shoveling through the dirt until you find the answers that lie somewhere under the unmarked graves of our comrades."

∞

On the drive back, Dan's mind traveled to a hundred places, but one thought stayed in the front of his brain. Something bothered Dan about Toby Waterson beyond the fact that he had called him "Joshua" there at the end. As a young man preparing to spread the word of God, he seemed too anxious to restore the legacies of his ancestors.

Mary Jo jumped into his mind. How would he explain to her that he had met another old soul from the South? Dead men from Gettysburg were coming back to life.

But there was another matter with a dead man that Dan needed to address.

He was going to visit his father.

June 28 – 10 a.m.

On the two-hour trek to Resurrection Cemetery in Piscataway, New Jersey, Dan realized he was driving back to a once-forgotten time and place. He hadn't been to the cemetery since that Christmas ago when his sister had asked him to help her lay a blanket of pine branches upon their father's and mother's plots.

While she had prayed over the graves, he had looked across the street and watched a man struggling in his front yard with a huge blow-up Santa Claus. Dan had excused himself to go and help the guy put up his decoration. When he had returned, his sister's scorn had been obvious.

Today he took baby steps onto the paved path at the entrance to the cemetery as if he was going to see his father alive, lying there, looking up, wondering who this strange sixty-year-old man was standing over him. Something pulled Dan along to the row where his father's headstone stood, the fourth one in from the left.

Joseph Michael Bryant
Born November 19, 1917
Died August 21, 1970

Dan looked down at his mother's headstone. He thought that if life after death healed all suffering, then he needed to believe that his mother and father had finally found peace with each other.

He had waited until everyone had left the house yesterday before sitting down with pen and paper at the kitchen table to write a letter to his father. After every other word, it seemed, he had stopped to think of what to write next.

Dan reached for the folded envelope in his back pocket and lifted out the letter. He fought back that feeling of being ten years old again looking up with hopeless anger at his father. Instead, he stood before the headstone and began to read.

> Dear Dad,
>
> It has taken me forty years to have the courage to write this letter to you.
>
> I can finally push my anger aside and see you as a man who could not be a father to me. I no longer blame you for that.
>
> I know you and Mom wanted to have a happy family long before I came along. Sickness stole your heart from me before you had any chance to give me your love.
>
> Thinking of you now makes me realize what a privilege I have to be a father to my children.
>
> Dad, I promise that I will be the man that you could not be. Your legacy will be my legacy.
>
> I can still make you proud.
>
> Your loving son,
> Danny

He returned the letter to the envelope and placed it on the grave. Joshua flashed into his mind, and Dan felt the urge to repeat a sentence he had just read. "I promise I will be the man that you could not be."

Dan smiled to himself, thinking that his old soul could still swing a bat to help him win the game of life.

"Excuse me, sir."

Dan turned to see a black man, looking very much like Morgan Freeman, dressed in overalls and holding a rake in his hands.

"Other than flowers, the cemetery forbids the placement of any objects upon the graves," the man said gently.

Dan swallowed back a confrontational remark when he saw the kindness that emanated from the man's deep green eyes.

"In this case, however," the old man said, while leaning his chin on the handle of the rake, "you may leave your envelope because I get the impression you haven't been here for a long time. You're certainly not one of our regulars."

"Thank you. I appreciate that. I was twenty-one the last time I was here. Just by looking at me, I'm sure you can tell that a lot of years have passed."

"Oh well, this is the best place to be if you want to talk about years passing." The man leaned forward against the rake. "I've been tending this cemetery for thirty-two years now. People come here every day to talk to the dead. Just the other day, Ol' Mr. Wilson made his one thousandth visit to his wife Louise. He brought a bottle of champagne to celebrate the occasion. I shared a glass with him."

He turned his attention back to Dan. "Do you talk to the dead?"

"Well, I really don't get the opportunity much," Dan replied, deciding not to reveal his connection to Joshua Park.

"I talk to the dead every day," the man said. "Oh, I know their souls don't stay here, but I'm believin' they come by whenever we're a-callin' to them." He shaded his eyes from the sun and pointed across the tops of white marble. "There's Harold over there in row 14. He's our oldest resident. Died in 1791. Can you even imagine what that man saw in his lifetime? He was just a baby during the American Revolution. Sometimes, when I think about how fast our technology is moving, I tell Harold we come a long way since ol' Ben Franklin flew that kite in a lightnin' storm."

He wiped the sweat off his brow.

"Then there's Melanie Baker over there in row 44. Poor girl was raped and murdered twenty years ago. Never got to see twenty years of life. It was all over the papers. Her mother used to come here ever' mornin' about ten. One day, I stopped by, and we had a chat. The guy that did it is in jail for life. She didn't care about that. Wasn't bringing her daughter back. She went on to tell me what a beautiful girl Melanie was, funny and bright, full of smiles and always looking forward to somethin' good."

The caretaker puckered his lips.

"I told Melanie's mom she needed to live by those words to honor her daughter. So I didn't see her for a long while. Then one day, there she was in the grocery store. She was wearing a T-shirt with a picture of Melanie, and under her daughter's face were the words 'Look forward to somethin' good.' She said she wouldn't be comin' by the cemetery no more."

He began to rake the leaves from the grave next to Dan's father.

"Then we got little Billy Jackson in row 18. Poor boy died of cancer at just eight years old. That was in the papers, too. Since his funeral, I never seen nobody come to his grave. Too painful, I guess. I still go over there and talk to Billy. The paper said he fought that damn disease for the last year of his life. It said wherever he would go with his family, people had sad faces for him, but Billy would get 'em laughin' in no time when he got 'em to play with his imaginary characters.

"There's a man who works down the street. He showed up at Billy's grave one day. Never even met the boy. He said he heard the stories about the full life Billy lived in just eight short years. The man told me the kid changed his life. He stopped drinkin' and started payin' more attention to his own kids. You see how the dead can help us be alive?" He looked into Dan's eyes with a shrewd gaze.

"I guess it's good when you talk to the dead because they don't talk back," Dan said.

"Oh, they talk back, just not out loud," he said. "You can *feel* their words here." The caretaker patted his heart. "No matter how young or old they were or how long they been dead, they're still doin' their thing to keep us livin' everyday, if you know what I mean.'

He looked across the lines of headstones.

"Nobody really goes away forever, you know. I descend from a long line of folks, right back to the days of slavery. Don't know where most are buried, but no matter. I can find my Uncle Gus whenever I think of him. Ma died when I was in grade school, but I still talk to her ever' day. She helps me carry on with my purpose, like talkin' to you today."

Slavery, thought Dan. Something stirred inside him. He had to ask the question. "So why are you telling me all this?"

"You ever hear of a lightworker?" The caretaker's easy grin relaxed the muscles that had tensed inside Dan's shoulders. "We help people find what they need to know."

Dan was puzzled. "Forgive my ignorance, but how do you become a lightworker?"

The man removed his gloves and put his right hand on Dan's shoulder. "I don't usually say that word because it can frighten some people. You see, I don't have no certificate from no school. When I put my faith in God, I learned that what I been doin' all along is the answer to the question to why he put me in this world."

Dan needed to interrupt. "Did you know I was coming here?"

"The moment I seen you, I said to myself that you came here for your daddy, but there's another journey that brought you here, too, and that's to get some advice. What you need to know about yourself ain't in no book or in no school. You follow the light from the spirits, and they gonna guide you to what you need to know."

"Spirits will help me?" Dan asked. "How am I supposed to know who they are?"

"You'll know. You'll feel them inside you and outside you, too. Follow their lead. They know you been chosen."

"Chosen?" Dan pondered that thought without much understanding.

"I must be goin' now," said the man. "Got work to do. First, I got to stop by and welcome Mrs. Francis over in row 27. She just arrived yesterday." His face opened into an ear-to-ear smile. "I wanna make sure she's comfortable."

Before Dan could ask again why he was chosen, the man walked away. After passing several headstones, he stopped and turned around. "That man down there in front of you is still your daddy." He pointed at Dan with the handle of the rake. "Talk to him. He's ready to give you back the love he couldn't give you before. And keep your faith. Like Melanie, you look forward to somethin' good, you hear?"

The man walked farther away, carrying the rake on his shoulder. Dan watched him until he seemed to disappear into the horizon.

As Dan looked down at his father's headstone, it wasn't his father who flashed through his mind. From somewhere came a vision of another black man from a different place from a time long ago. "Never lose faith, son," said Joseph Charles. "When all else fails us, faith is all we got left."

June 28 – 2 p.m.

Before Dan could put two feet into the house, Mary Jo stood at the edge of the doorway blocking his entrance.

"Wait until you hear what your son was doing today!"

"Something tells me you're going to inform me now, so I won't have to wait." Dan walked up to Mary Jo. He tried to kiss her on the cheek, but she pulled away.

"This is serious, Dan," she said. "Katy told me that when she let the dogs out, she saw Jacob and Jessie kissing behind the big willow tree in her backyard."

Dan broke into song: "Jessie and Jacob sittin' in a tree, k-i-s-s-i-n—"

"Stop it, Dan. This is serious."

"Okay. If they were fully clothed and if their hands weren't where they shouldn't be, then what's the big deal?"

"Dan, they're fifteen. Remember when you were fifteen with your hormones raging? A kiss today makes a baby tomorrow!"

"Now, that would've been big news for me back in my day. First of all, I never got to kiss Miss Wilson, my hot Spanish teacher, and even if I had, I don't think she would have wanted to have a baby with a confused pimply faced teenager who, besides thinking about sex all the time, was a never-going-to-happen Major League baseball player."

"Dan, when I confronted Jacob, he ran upstairs and slammed his bedroom door. I told him not to come out until I said so."

"Should I have a birds-and-bees talk with him?" Dan asked.

"That would be great coming from a man who's told me that every erection should be a shared activity, whether it be in the bedroom, the bathroom, or the front seat of his car." Mary Jo shook her head and walked into the kitchen to prepare dinner. Dan followed her.

"Well now," he reacted, "you and I have nicely fulfilled those requirements, haven't we? We should also throw in the state park, a swimming pool, and let's not forget the behind-the-center-field fence after the softball game was over and they turned off the lights. You had those short shorts on, and after you gave me that look, I just reached around in front and—"

"Enough, Dan. You're always thinking with the wrong head."

"I bet that's what my mother said to my father on the night they made me." He picked this spot to mention his dad. "You know he spoke to me from his grave—where I went today, remember?" Dan regretted saying that. He didn't want to make Mary Jo feel guilty because she didn't ask about his trip to the cemetery.

"I get it, Dan. I know what you're trying to do with that remark. You want to play my game? I thought we had crossed that bridge. Before your son makes that little girl next door ask someone at school about an abortion, you and he and your dear departed dad should sing a couple of verses of 'The Cat's in the Cradle.'"

"I spend time with Jacob, Mary Jo."

"Sure you do. If it weren't for the baseball season, you might wonder who that strange boy is passing you in the hall to go to the bathroom. Warm up the leftovers. I need a break."

She left the room. This time there was no slam of the bedroom door.

∞

Before he knocked on Jacob's bedroom door, Dan asked his father to help him say the right words.

"Jacob, can I come in?"

He heard a video game go silent, followed by a weak "yeah" from Jacob.

Dan entered and sat down on the bed alongside his son. "Your mother told me what happened today between you and Jessie."

No response departed from Jacob's mouth. He stared at a frozen zombie on the TV screen.

"We aren't upset; we're just a little concerned about what your behavior with her will be from this point forward."

Jacob kept his eyes on the screen.

"I mean, the wedding isn't supposed to happen for a long while yet, and if you get tired of kissing her before then, you guys just might not make it."

Jacob turned his eyes to Dan, who could see that his attempt at humor was not working.

"You mean like you and Mom?" he asked flatly.

"Mom and I are fine. I know you've seen us argue a lot lately, mostly because of something that's going on in my head, but we're working through all that."

"She thinks you're crazy and that you don't pay much attention to Katy and me anymore." A sadness shadowed Jacob's face.

"Well, let me tell you what I learned today from a man I had never met before today and will most likely never see again. I'm understanding myself better so I can be a better father and husband, and I think I'm pretty close to figuring it out. This man told me there will be more helpers, too, who will be guiding me along."

"Mom said you think you're some soldier guy who died in the Civil War. That sounds like you're crazy to me."

"Don't worry about me, Jacob. I'll figure this thing out, and then everything will be the way it used to be with our family."

"Dad, we kissed *once*. Bratty Katy got Mom all upset over nothing."

"Katy saw something that upset her, that's all." Dan refocused the subject matter. "How was it? The kiss, I mean. How did it make you feel?"

"I don't know. It was okay, I guess."

∞

"Just one piece of advice before I go." Dan placed his hands on each of Jacob's shoulders. "With young ladies, stay ahead in the game. Keep them trying to catch up. Once they get the lead, you're done, game over. Then they want to play against somebody else."

Jacob smiled.

Dan hugged and held onto his son, thinking how fast the years had passed since Daddy had held baby Jake for his midnight feeding.

"Dad, when you figure that other thing out, you know about the soldier and all, will you tell me?"

"I promise you'll know everything. In the meantime, stay away from that willow tree for a while. You know Mom's going to be spying through the window."

"But Jessie and I really like that tree. It's our favorite place to talk about things." He picked up the game controller. "What was your name back then, in the war?"

"Joshua Park," Dan replied. "I had a girlfriend, too. Her name was Becky. Just like you and Jessie, we liked to sit under a big ol' tree."

Dan stood up to leave. Jacob looked at him as if he wanted to say something, yet nothing came from his mouth. As Dan walked to the doorway, he threw a curious glance back at his son, who had already resumed killing video zombies.

June 28 – 10 p.m.

With his restless legs kicking again, Dan sat outside on a front porch chair. A moonless starry night formed a canopy above him. He recalled a poster he had placed above his bed when he was a teenager, a picture of the night sky, illuminated by hundreds of tiny white stars. Below the stars on a bench sat a man looking upward. The caption at the bottom of the poster read, "How many nights must a man look up at the sky before he can see the stars?"

His memory led to a time when Eddie Rose came over one day to listen to the Allman Brothers' new album.

❧

"I don't get it," said Eddie, staring at the poster.

"This song?" Danny asked.

"Why can't he see the damn stars? He's looking right at them!"

That was Eddie's problem. To him, everything said or written was brutally literal. In a baseball game one afternoon, Eddie swung at a pitch and hit a fast ground ball into left field that never bounced once off the ground. Their coach had called Eddie's hit a "worm burner."

In between innings, Eddie bent over and walked along the path his base hit had taken.

"Eddie, what are you doing?" Danny asked.

"Looking for burning worms, but I don't see any, do you?"

"Burning worms? What are you talking about?"

"My hit was a worm burner. I guess there should be some smoke too."

"That's just a baseball expression," Danny explained. "It means the ball stayed close to the ground and never bounced up."

Eddie looked confused.

"There aren't any worms, Eddie. Coach meant that if there were worms and you hit the ball that way, then—oh, never mind."

An inning later, a batter hit an easy fly ball to the outfield. The coach yelled, "A can of corn!" as the ball settled into Eddie's glove.

When they came to the bench, Eddie sat down next to Danny. After Jimmy Flint singled to start the inning, Eddie asked, "Where's the corn Coach was yelling about?"

"Right next to that piece of cake," Danny answered as they watched Jimmy Flint slide safely into second with a stolen base.

⚊

Eddie vanished from Dan's mind. He was replaced by a very clear image of Joshua Park. Dan zoomed in his focus ring. Curls of blond hair protruded from both sides of Joshua's gray cap. Small light-red lips appeared to be tightly closed. His cheeks were pale, defined by angles of approaching manhood. Steel-blue eyes defined a boy who had lost his childhood innocence to fight in a war that demanded he be a man.

Dan wondered why he didn't know everything about Joshua. Did they have similar thoughts when they were teenagers? Did they share the wrong ideas about sex? Were they one and the same in their beliefs about the spiritual world outside the little boxes they lived in?

All these questions led Dan to wonder if he really was reincarnated as this Southern boy or just watching a mind movie about the kid put there by some mystical force. It really didn't matter, Dan thought. *It is what it is.*

Then a new idea came to Dan as to why he and Joshua were bonded together. They both put their faith into the only reason why life was worth living.

To be in love.

Joshua vanished in the next second. Dan glanced up at the deep black sky, littered by twinkling stars that were dancing to the inaudible music of the heavens. He remembered a Walt Whitman poem about a student who became bored in an astronomy class with all the analytical diagrams and scientific explanations of the bodies of matter that surround the moon. The student left the class and walked outside to look up into the sky. He marveled not about the physical matter of the stars but about their incredible mysticism.

From somewhere, a voice charged through Dan's head.

Clay County! Clay County!

"I have to go to Clay County, Alabama?" Dan asked, staring up at the stars.

"Dan! Dan! Help me, Dan!"

Joshua? No! It wasn't Joshua. The voice came from inside the house.

"Dan!" screamed Mary Jo from the bedroom.

He bolted off the porch, threw the door open, and rushed up the stairs. Katy stood at the bedroom doorway, sobbing between deep breaths. Jacob turned to face Dan from the edge of the bed. Mary Jo clutched her knees to her chest.

"Dad, is Mom going to die?" Jacob asked with a shake in his words.

"Mary Jo. Talk to me. What's wrong?"

"Ahhhh. Pain. The pain!" She grabbed her stomach with both hands.

Dan lifted the phone and dialed Mike and Diana next door. Six or seven rings later, Mike picked up. "Mike, Dan. Listen, I have to take Mary Jo to the hospital. She's in a lot of pain. Can you or Diana come watch the kids? I know Jacob is old enough to stay with Katy, but I don't want them to be by themselves. Thanks, Mike. I'm sorry about calling you this late. I really appreciate this."

"Dad. I can watch Katy," said Jacob in a tone of disappointment.

"I know, I know, son, but I'd rather have Mike stay with you until we get back. Please try to keep Katy from being scared."

"Are you scared, Dad?"

"Yes, I'm scared. It's okay to be scared until we find out what's wrong."

Mary Jo rolled her body back and forth with her eyes shut.

Mike was already at the door.

"Jacob," Dan said, "go let him in."

Katy ran into Dan's open arms.

"Mommy is going to be fine, Katy."

"I'm scared, Daddy." She buried her tear-drenched face in Dan's stomach.

"I promise I'll take care of her. I need you to believe me."

"Okay, Daddy," she said through her sobs.

Mike appeared at the bedroom doorway. "What's wrong, Dan?" he asked.

Mary Jo's moaning became louder.

"I don't know. She's in too much pain to tell me. Help me get her up."

They tried to lift Mary Jo from the bed. "No!" she screamed. Katy cried louder. Jacob stepped back and wiped tears from the corners of his eyes.

"Call for an ambulance," said Mike. "They can give her something for the pain so we can move her."

June 29 – Around Midnight

Dan sat next to Mary Jo amidst spinning lights and ear-piercing sirens. The ambulance raced toward Gnaden Huetten Memorial Hospital in Lehighton. Along the way, Dan kept trying to chase Jacob's words from his mind.

Is Mom going to die?

As they ran Mary Jo down the hall on a gurney, Dan followed behind. The EMTs wouldn't risk a prognosis, other than to say she had acute abdominal discomfort. She was given a shot to take the edge off the pain. Her vitals were stable.

Turning at the end of a hall, they rolled her through a set of doors. A nurse stopped Dan and told him to wait in a visitor's room to the left. She told him that as soon as they knew anything, he would be the first to know.

Dan called Mary Jo's sister who would inform his mother-in-law. He sat down next to a woman who was staring at the ceiling. Dropping his face in his hands, he couldn't help but let his mind go back to Jacob's words.

Is Mom going to die?

Time passed, an hour or so.

Dan picked up an old magazine, but his brain rattled with thoughts of raising two kids without their mother. *Never mind. It's going to be nothing at all.* Food poisoning? No, they had all eaten the same chicken for dinner. Kidney stone? That might be it.

"Mr. Bryant, I'm Doctor Morehead."   A man in scrubs stood at the doorway. "Can I see you in the hall for a minute?"

Dan bounced up from his chair, nearly tripping over the lady who was still staring at the ceiling.

"Mr. Bryant, an MRI scan located a large mass on your wife's right ovary that was pressing against the abdominal wall."

A lump formed instantly in Dan's throat. He somehow forced questions though it. "A mass? Is it a tumor?"

"Yes. It's quite large, about the size of a baseball. We have recommended that she have it removed along with the ovary as soon as possible."

"How soon?"

"She's given her consent, but she'd like to speak with you first. We can begin the procedure within the hour."

Dan's head exploded with questions that he didn't have time to ask.

"You can come in now and see her, Mr. Bryant. She's resting comfortably. We gave her something for the pain."

As they walked toward her room, Dan grabbed Dr. Morehead by his shoulder. "Could this be cancer?" he asked.

"We won't have a diagnosis until we get a report from the pathology lab. We should get a response before the sun comes up."

Mary Jo greeted Dan with a weak smile. "Hey, old man," she said through a graveled voice. "Shouldn't this be the other way around, you lying here and me standing there?"

"If I could trade places with you, I would in a heartbeat." He bent over and kissed her softly on her lips.

"Who's with the kids?"

"Mike is being relieved by your mom. I'm sure she's with them by now. I told your mom I would call her. She wants to be here."

"She can come after you leave and I get out of recovery." She looked up at the bright white light over her bed. "So . . . I guess you heard. I've been carrying around a baseball on my ovary for a while. Have you been throwing curveballs inside me, or what?"

"No, I only throw screwballs."

Mary Jo struggled to let out a laugh. "Well, next time throw me . . . what do you call that slow pitch?"

"A change of pace," said Dan.

"Throw me a change of pace so I know it's coming, And next time, throw it outside the strike zone."

"It's amazing what that drug did to your body. Pain-free and mouth free. It's great to have you back," said Dan.

She grabbed his hand. "We have to get this out. There's no other option. Dr. Morehead said it's a pretty simple procedure, but as with all surgeries, there are risks."

"I agree, honey," said Dan with a reassuring smile. "You'll be fine. I just know it."

Her eyes filled with tears. "I'll count on that," she said. "After all, you've been telling me for the past sixteen years that you know everything."

"And I haven't been wrong yet."

Dr. Morehead walked into the room. "It's time, Mrs. Bryant."

Mary Jo reached for Dan's hand again. "As soon as I get better, I want to help you figure out this Joshua Park thing so we can get on with our lives."

"I'll take you up on that." Dan kissed her cheek. "Maybe a trip to Alabama will help."

"Only if you wear a red football helmet with a white stripe. I never told you, but I got a thing for men wearing head gear."

"And I got a thing for cheerleaders. We'll have to pass the kids off to your mom for a football dress rehearsal."

With more tears filling her eyes, Mary Jo mouthed three words that traveled straight to his heart. He threw her a hand kiss as she disappeared into the hall.

Dan returned to the waiting room that was empty now. He slumped into a chair and did something he hadn't done in years. He began to pray.

"She's in recovery. Everything went just fine," said Dr. Morehead. "She'll be asleep for a while, so when she wakes, a nurse will come get you."

"Any guesses about the tumor—I mean, the mass?" asked Dan.

"I don't want to say anything that might be discredited by the pathology report, but its texture was more liquid than solid. That's usually a good sign, but we'll have to get the report. We should know in a few hours."

∞

A few hours passed. The sun had poked a few fingers of light though the dusty blinds on the waiting-room window. Dan had checked on Mary Jo twice. She was still asleep.

Dr. Morehead appeared at the doorway again. "We have the report back." He stared down at the paper with what Dan thought was a concerned look upon his face.

"So, what's the deal?" asked Dan.

"The lab determined that the tumor was 'borderline malignant.'"

"Borderline malignant? What exactly does that mean?" asked Dan, with an edge in his in his voice.

"It means that it has the potential to be malignant, but it may not be."

"Is it cancer? Almost cancer? Not cancer? What?" Dan's anger was surfacing.

"We've ordered a second test to see if we can be more definitive. The good news for now is that we cannot for certain call it a malignancy."

Dan lowered his eyes to the floor. He shuffled his feet across the tiles.

Dr. Morehead placed his hand upon Dan's shoulder. "Look. I understand your anxiety over this uncertainty, but hopefully we'll find a better answer shortly. In the meantime, be there for Mary Jo when she wakes up. Don't tell her anything until I get the second report, and don't tell anyone in your family just yet." He patted Dan's shoulder.

When Dan lifted his eyes off the floor, Dr. Morehead had already disappeared down the hall.

After checking on Mary Jo again, Dan found her still asleep. He took the elevator down to the cafeteria. Thoughts of gloom and doom filled his head.

Cancer. Months of radiation and chemotherapy. For what? Her grandmother went through the whole mess. Hair loss. Weight loss. Then remission. Then it came back, and she died anyway. Then again, maybe it's not cancer. Maybe Mary Jo will just have to be careful. Get frequent checkups .Get a complete hysterectomy.

Dan had always been a worst-case-scenario kind of guy. He resolved to avoid that tendency this time. If she had to fight the disease, he would step up to the plate and take care of her and the kids.

He stood in line waiting to pay for a plastic-wrapped donut when someone tapped him on his shoulder. He turned around to see a woman dressed in a blue nurse's uniform. She had dark-brown hair pulled back from a face that was aged with lines and wrinkles. She smiled at him, a smile that delivered a certain aura of peace about her. "Excuse me, sir," she said. "You don't have anything to worry about. Your wife will be fine."

Dan narrowed his eyes. "Are you one of her nurses? I haven't seen you around her. How would you know? Is the second report back from pathology already?"

"No, I'm not her nurse. And I didn't see any report."

"Then . . . what are you telling me?" Dan tried not to think that this woman was a nut job who had sneaked into the hospital wearing a nurse's outfit.

"Please don't think I'm crazy or giving you false hope. Call it my intuition. When I walked by her room, I stopped and looked in. My mind got this strong sense that it's not her time yet. She's a strong-willed lady who has a lot of life left to live. She'll take care of her peeps and you too, Mr. Bryant. God's not taking her home for a long while."

How dare you say these things just because you looked in on her!

"There's an old saying, Mr. Bryant. 'Those who bleed red, sleep sound in their bed.' Trust me. I just know that what I'm telling you is true. Your wife is a strong, red-blooded woman. She will have many stories to share with her grandkids, and many will be about you, Mr. Bryant. She'll have a lot to experience with you in the next few years that will bring the two of you closer together."

Just like that, she turned and walked away. Dan stood frozen to the floor. He looked down into his hands. He had squeezed the donut to mush. As he watched her turn the corner, his mind brought back the words she had said:

Those who bleed red, sleep sound in their bed.

Somewhere, sometime, he had heard those words before. Joshua Park suddenly appeared in his mind. This time, he wore no gray uniform and looked younger than nineteen. He was lying in his bed, and his mother was with him in the room.

Then they both disappeared from his mind as quickly as they had arrived.

The nurse said Mary Jo would take care of her "peeps." How did she know about Katy and Jacob, and why did she call them "peeps"? *How did she know I was Mr. Bryant?*

Dan threw a dollar on the counter and ran down the hall to find her. Walking toward him was another nurse.

"Excuse me," Dan said while catching his breath. "Do you know a nurse with dark brown hair pulled back, kind of middle aged? She just went down this hall."

"Did you notice her name tag?" she asked.

"I didn't look close enough to see a last name," Dan said, "but her first name was Martha. "

"I've been the head nurse here for sixteen years, and the only one who comes to mind is Martha Hyatt, but she retired maybe fifteen years ago—and I heard she died recently. We have a much younger group on this shift today. I think Audrey may be the oldest, and she's not much past thirty, with blond hair, too."

An awkward moment of silence came between them.

"Sorry I couldn't be of any help," she said. "I have a call I have to attend to. Maybe you spoke to an orderly or a cafeteria worker, and you were mistaken about the uniform." The nurse walked away, leaving Dan standing there with his hands on his hips.

"No, she was no orderly or cafeteria worker," he said aloud. He thought about what the lightworker had said in the cemetery. Could she have been one of the spirit guides he had talked about?

Dan hurried to the elevator. Mary Jo should be awake by now.

June 29 – 2:30 a.m.

Dan's feet barely touched the floor when he walked into Mary Jo's room. An overwhelming sense of calm had overcome all his anxieties. Despite being awake all night long, he felt lifted by a new energy, as if his body had been hooked up to a garden hose that flushed cool water through his veins.

He found Dr. Morehead at her bedside.

"It's about time you showed up," said Mary Jo. "Did you forget I was here?"

"Actually I did," said Dan. "I was wandering the halls looking for the cameras filming *ER*. This must not be that hospital. The nurses here aren't as pretty as the ones on the TV show." He took her hand in his. "Then, all of a sudden, my senior moment ended, and I remembered I was married to Sleeping Beauty in here."

"Well, then, you're not Prince Phillip," she said. "You didn't even wait at the door of my recovery room. There was once a time when you wouldn't let me out of your sight."

"Now that I'm here, let's not waste the good doctor's time and see what he has to say."

"You missed that too," said Mary Jo.

"The second report came back," said Dr. Morehead. "The results are the same as the first. The tumor is borderline malignant."

"Which side of the line are we on?" asked Dan.

"We can be clear that she does *not* have cancer, nor will she have to receive typical cancer treatments. We will, however, have to monitor her body closely. I'll be referring Mary Jo to a gynecological oncologist."

"I knew it," said Dan.

"Knew what?" Mary Jo asked. "That I'd have to see a cancer doctor?"

"That you'd be fine. Someone stopped me downstairs and— never mind. Just intuition, I guess."

"Dr. Morehead, why a cancer doctor?" she asked.

"He'll schedule periodic tests of your reproductive and digestive systems because the tumor is described as intestinal in nature."

"Dr. Morehead says I'll have to get yearly colonoscopies as part of my routine check-ups," said Mary Jo. "You and I can have them together, Dan. You're of that age anyway, and what better way to share our love than to spend the night before the test texting each other from toilet bowls across the house?"

"Don't you just love her?" Dan smiled at the doctor. "I've learned that the most important thing in our relationship is my sense of humor. Whether what she says is funny or not, I laugh now. I have no other choice. Besides, I love her too much to take anything she says seriously."

"Well then, I should thank you for thinking I'm nothing but a joke." Mary Jo reached out for his hand.

"I've got some rounds to make, " Dr. Morehead said looking down at his clipboard. "I'll see you tomorrow morning around nine."

Dan shook the doctor's hand. "Thank you," said Dan. "We're so glad we caught this thing relatively early."

With a nod of his head, the doctor disappeared into the hall.

"*We* got this thing early?" Mary Jo frowned. "I don't remember you screaming along with me from the bed a few hours ago."

"Listen. I have it from a spiritual authority that you're going to live to a very old age."

"Oh, you're talking to God now? Ask him to help you drum up a recipe for Southern fried chicken from back in your Alabama days. I'll be hungry for some good and greasy finger food when I get home."

"You're sharp tonight. No hangover from the anesthesia, obviously."

"Kiss me now while I still have one ovary left," she said. "If the next one goes, I might lose any desire I have left for you, old man."

Dan put his lips upon hers, a kiss that skipped a beat in his heart, just as the first one had done so many years ago.

Throughout July

Midsummer fell upon Dan like magic dust from Tinker Bell's wand. Mary Jo recovered well enough to plant her rose garden. Over morning coffee, they watched hummingbirds drink nectar from a feeder attached to the window above the kitchen sink. Afternoons brought about family trips to a near-by pristine mountain lake where Katy built sand castles on the shoreline while Jacob pretended he wasn't texting Jessie. Once Jessie came with them, and Dan witnessed that typical teenage thing: Jacob chased Jessie through the water's edge before they competed in a volleyball game while half-submerged in the lake. This event, of course, was played through a constant, friendly argument over the rules and who scored what number of points.

Despite acting their ages, Jacob and Jessie were proving to be much more than teenage crushes, not by the way they spoke or acted but by the way they looked into each other's eyes—lasting, sincere, holding an unspoken promise to someday meet at the altar for a couple of "I dos," or so Dan believed.

Cool summer evenings beckoned the family to Dan's prize possession, his outdoor fire table. The sound of music floated from an iPod through the night air, warmed by the radiance of the fire. One night, inspired by the rhythm of the leaping flames, Dan reminisced with Mary Jo about the special times he'd enjoyed with Jacob.

Father and son were spending a few days fishing together in the lake from an aluminum boat. On one particular muggy morning, Jacob reeled in a six-pound largemouth bass.

"You want to keep it?" asked Dan.

"I don't want to eat it," replied Jacob, as Dan held it up for a cell phone picture.

"We could get it mounted."

"That would be cool."

"Let's call him Robert E. Lee," said Dan.

"Why?"

"You must have learned about him in history class. Lee surrendered after a long and difficult fight."

"I get it," said Jacob, looking at the bass flopping on the stringer.

When they got home, Dan removed the fish, which he had shoved head first into a bait bucket of water. He laid it on the lawn and started to unload the rest of the car.

"Why did you put it there?"

The bass was flapping side to side, its red gills flaring in futile attempts to breathe.

"Jacob, the fish has to die before I can put it into the freezer." Dan studied the expression on his son's face. "There's still time if we hurry."

"Let's go, Dad."

Back into the bucket the fish went, and back to the lake Dan drove his son. They ran Robert E. Lee to the water's edge. Holding the bass by its mouth and tail, Dan carefully lowered it into the water. He moved the big fish back and forth until it wiggled free and swam off.

"Thanks, Dad," Jacob said with a gasp of relief.

"I never really wanted to put him on the wall anyway," said Dan. "We let him go for fighting the great fight."

"Dad, Lee was your Civil War general, right?"

"Yes, son. And even though the South lost the war, he's still a hero down there."

Jacob skipped a stone across the surface of the lake. "What can you tell me about your girlfriend? Her name was Becky, right?"

"She just took me by surprise, as your mother did."

"How did he know—how did *you* know? Do you know what I'm trying to say, Dad?"

"Let me see if I can explain, son. With Joshua—I mean, with Becky and me and with your mother and me, we didn't begin with love at first sight. In fact, it was more like a second or third look, now that I think about it. After some time—and it takes time, son—you just kind of know. You just kind of feel it. You just kind of, I don't know, you just know."

Jacob shot a puzzled glance at Dan, as if his attempt at defining love had missed the strike zone with a wild pitch.

Dan decided to throw him a changeup. "So what can you tell me about *your* girlfriend?"

With a deep breath, Jacob sat back. "When I think about Jessie, what you said kind of makes sense. We tried not liking each other. We even tried liking somebody else, but to be honest, we've come to realize that we do like each other; we just never say it." Jacob dragged his feet over the stones in the parking lot as they walked back to the car. "Yesterday when we sat under the tree, she said something really weird to me."

"Weird?"

"She said we were meant for each other, and there's nothing we can do to change that."

"Well, I can tell you this about my experience with women," said Dan. "When they want something, they'll do whatever it takes to get it and keep it."

Jacob didn't talk again until Dan pulled the car into the garage. "Gotta go, Dad. Promised Jessie I'd help her plant a flower garden behind the tree."

As he walked toward the door, Dan called out to get his attention. "One more thing, son. Don't bother trying to figure them out. Just go along with the mood of the moment."

"Like you did with that girl, Becky, and with Mom?" Jacob asked.

Dan opened his mouth, but he couldn't speak a word. His son had come to the realization that his father not only had two lives but also was in love with two women. *Now that's something Jacob better not tell his teammates at the next baseball game.*

The next morning, Dan placed a paper cutout of a large-mouth bass next to Jacob's cereal bowl. He added a word balloon next to the fish's head. Inside the balloon, he wrote the words, "Thanks for letting me live!" and signed Robert E. Lee across its tail.

∽

"Not just another fish story," Dan said to Mary Jo. Another catch-and-release activity between a father and his son was even more special than casting out lines from a boat.

What Dan enjoyed doing most with Jacob was tossing a baseball back and forth. The intricacies of this one-act play performed on a backyard stage proved that the rewards of having a catch with his son had little to do with throwing him a ball. The sound, the scent, and the sight of this simple event added together equaled the sum of their souls. The thumping of the ball against their gloves resonated like a native drumbeat, an awakening of a lost childhood for Dan and the emerging of a young manhood for Jacob. In between throws, they stood tall, facing each other, holding gloves to their noses as if they were raising glasses for a toast.

The spinning white sphere delivered words of endearment in silent voices with every sling of their arms.

"You are my dad," Jacob exclaimed to his father each time he threw him the ball.

"You are my son," Dan sent sailing to Jacob with every return throw.

The repeated ritual marked a giving and receiving of their love, along with the passing of a tradition from one generation to another. Dan hoped that if his son became a father someday, he would grab his baseball glove each time he heard his own boy ask the one question that invites an opportunity for a dad to authenticate his fatherhood in the eyes of his adoring child.

"Hey, Dad, you wanna play catch?"

After one of these special ceremonies with Jacob, Dan sat down with him over glasses of iced tea.

"So, Mom tells me she hasn't had any further reports of you and Jessie lip-locked under the willow tree," he said lightly.

"Daa-aaad," said Jacob with a whine in his voice. "We still go there, but, you know, we just talk."

"Well that's good, but if you need to sneak in a smooch every now and then, just stay away from windows." Dan threw a soft punch into Jacob's arm. "Son, with all kidding aside, is Jessie really still that special to you?"

"I want to ask her to the kickoff dance when school starts again. It's not just that I think she's pretty, but when we hang out in her backyard, we talk about things that we both say never come up with anyone else."

"So what do you talk about, if I may ask?"

"Just stuff. About everything around us. I mean, we look at nature and how it works together. Jessie wonders who figures this all out. I say, it just happens."

"What else?"

"Well, the other day she wondered why we were born in the first place and why we're born to our parents, rather than to different parents. I told her I guess it just happens that way, just like nature. I said all this makes us special. Look at the sky, the earth, and you realize how short human life can be. That means we shouldn't waste a minute and nature's gonna outlive us all."

"Did she agree?"

"Not really," said Jacob, lifting his eyes to the sky. "She agrees that the lives we live are short, but she thinks we can come back to live again in someone else's body. She thinks that a person's spirit can get passed along after it dies."

Jacob looked at his dad. "Like that Civil War kid. He passed his spirit to you." Dan took a breath. "If what Jessie says and what I'm going through are true, it could be a beautiful thing, like a dead flower that gets to bloom again."

"But Dad, but why were *you* picked? And does everyone get to have another life?"

"Those are questions I've asked myself a hundred times. I hope someday I'll find out the answers, or . . . I'll just have to live with the questions."

They sat in silence for a moment with Dan thinking their talk had ended. Then Jacob said, "My friend Billy says his dad never has time to play catch with him. He's always too busy." Jacob punched his fist into the pocket of his glove.

"That's sad," said Dan. "Let me tell you, son, from now on, no matter how busy I might be, I will make time for what matters most—and what matters most are the people I love and who love me back."

"So if you were a doctor and you were in the middle of an operation and I came by and asked you to play catch, would you drop everything and go get your glove?" Jacob asked.

Dan laughed. "Well, now, that gets into another thing I've always told you. Finish what you start, but keep your word. Play catch right after you do what you have to do."

"Dad, can I tell you about other stuff that was going through my head?"

"Absolutely."

"When I thought you were going crazy and you didn't know I was alive, I told myself not to care because it would make me too angry. Then Mom got sick, and I thought she was going to die, so I wondered, *What will we do without parents?* Katy cried a lot about these things. She was really scared. You never knew. Mom cried too, but then she got angry. I never saw her so upset."

"I made a mistake, son." Dan let out a sigh. "I was a terrible father and a lousy husband." He put his arm around Jacob. "You had every right to have those feelings. I am truly sorry for not being there for you and Katy, but Mom and I have climbed back up the mountain. We're a family again."

Jacob smiled. He put his arms around his father as he did when he was a little boy when Dan would say, "Give me a monster hug!" "Keep looking 'til you get all your answers, Dad—about that soldier, I mean. I think what you have to find out will be important to me, too."

Jacob jumped up and went to the back door where he turned and looked back. "If Jessie's right, then Joshua might get another chance to live," Jacob said. "Like Robert E. Lee."

August 4 – 1 a.m.

A night of restless legs sent Dan to the Internet. His *Mission: Impossible* assignment was to find anyone and everyone named Rebecca who had a recorded residence in Clay County, Alabama, within the last thirty years of the nineteenth century.

His research discovered two persons.

Rebecca Willow, born in 1844, daughter of Mary and Jonathan Willow, lived in the county from 1862 until her death in 1929. Rebecca Talley, born in 1847, died in 1910, had lived there as well. Dan could find no other information about either one.

The ridiculous odds of finding living relatives in Alabama made him think that going there would be a waste of time. To find ancestors would be one thing, but anyone who knew anything at all about Joshua Park's Becky would be even more incredible. Then again, his encounters with Toby Waterson, the lightworker, and the mysterious nurse had Dan believing that his search was guided and another helpful soul from Clay County might provide important clues about Becky Willow or Becky Talley.

A fourteen-hour drive of nearly nine hundred miles to probe around in somebody's private business didn't jump out as a great idea either, yet his on-again, off-again, now on-again obsession with young Mr. Park threw back the lack of logic to reform a clear and resounding point of direction in his head.

I have to do this.

The next night, Dan went into the bedroom to tell Mary Jo his plan.

"Can I talk to you about something?" he asked.

She lifted her head from a magazine. "I'm going with you," she said.

"What are you talking about?"

"I'll have my mother stay here with the kids. I told her just the other day that this would happen."

"But I haven't even—"

"We're going to Alabama together." Mary Jo fluffed the pillow behind her.

"I was thinking it might be better if I go alone." Dan climbed into bed.

"Listen—before my surgery, I told you that, from now on, your journey is my journey. After all, don't you think that Joshua might have had something to do with your choosing me to be your wife? I think I'm a player in his game, too." She smacked the side of his pillow. "So put me in the lineup, coach!"

"I always did have a thing for Southern ladies. It goes back a long time," he said.

"Well, I might like to see firsthand the sweaty muscles of a young buck while he works in the fields down there."

"Hmm," said Dan. "There's a role play in there somewhere."

"You have a dirty mind," she replied.

"Exactly. I was told I'd have to shovel through dirt to get to the bottom of all this, so let's go to the land of the Crimson Tide and see what we can dig up."

Dan plotted the travel route. They would stop for an overnight somewhere and then book a Holiday Express in Lineville, Clay County, for two nights. They would visit local municipal buildings and churches to search for records that might lead them to discover where the two Rebeccas had lived. He figured if they didn't find anything after a few days, they'd give it up and head back.

Mary Jo briefed her mother about how to manage the kids. She added an asterisk next to Jacob's name for the times he might be together with Jessie. Mom's ground rules could take up more pages than those in the Little League handbook: No this. No that. Curfews. Forbidden places, both indoors and outdoors. About the only thing she didn't prescribe was what they were allowed to talk about.

"I told my mom if Jacob brings Jessie into our house, they can watch TV in the family room. Of course, no video games in his room," she said.

"Is that because they would have to sit next to each other on the bed to play?" asked Dan.

"Stop it, Dan. You know how one thing can lead to another at their age."

"You're right. You start playing Call of Duty, and before long it gets so exciting, you just want to rip your clothes off."

Mary Jo was not fond of saying the F word, but Dan could see her lips shooting out a silent version toward him.

"Okay, okay," he said. "I'll remind him to act like a gentleman."

∞

With their bags packed, Dan kissed and hugged Katy, who then skipped into grandma's waiting arms. He waved his hand for Jacob to step outside the garage. "Just a word of advice, son."

"I know, Dad. Behave myself and don't do anything to disappoint you or Mom."

"Did you think of that all by yourself?"

"No. Mom said it for the third time five minutes ago."

Dan smiled and hugged Jacob. He whispered the words "monster hug" into his son's ear and got the big squeeze in return.

"I hope you come back with what you need to know," said Jacob.

"It's like trying to catch Robert E. Lee again," said Dan. "But as you said the other day, if I do hook him, I promise you I will let him live again."

∞

Seven hours into the drive, Dan pulled into the parking lot of a Comfort Inn just across the Tennessee border. The late summer sky hung heavy with hot, sticky air that reminded Dan of why he loved living in the cool Pocono Mountains of Jim Thorpe.

A dinner of Southern fried chicken and a few beers sent him and Mary Jo belly-full and bone-tired onto two weather-beaten Adirondack chairs at the back patio of the inn.

"This is a terrible time for me to say this," said Dan, "but why am I still chasing a ghost? I mean, what are the chances of us finding anything in Alabama 145 years after the fact?"

"Okay, so you came all the way down here, and now you need a pep talk?" Mary Jo asked. "Then I'm going to give you one."

Dan glanced over at Mary Jo and reached for her hand, which she slapped into his. "When I was finally convinced about Johnny Reb—excuse me, Joshua Park—I found so much more about you to be intriguing. Think about it, Dan. Our family heritage is depending on finding the answer to the question *why*. And need I remind you of all the help you've had directing you to Clay County? The reenactor, the man in the cemetery, the nurse in the hospital—there's no coincidence or imagined connections about them; they're real. This whole ridiculous story is not fiction. It's fact. It all points to coming here, right now. You have to trust a woman's intuition about this. Something will turn up."

Dan gazed up at the twilight of the evening sky, a mystical moment that inspires poets to rhyme, artists to create, and dreamers to imagine the unbelievable.

"Whether we complete this crazy story or not," he said, "we're completing something between us that was incomplete for too long."

"Did you make that up all by yourself?"

"I had some help from the light in the sky."

Later, under another mystical moment, they made love to the music of the night crickets outside their window.

August 11 – 6 p.m.

Dan and Mary Jo arrived in Lineville, Alabama, the next day just as the light in the sky faded into a soft gray. Once in the hotel room, Dan thought of an idea to kill off the night before they began their research in the morning.

"What do you say after we shower, we hit that club we passed and throw back a few?" he asked her. "I think it was called The Watering Hole."

"You want to see if Southern hospitality is fact or fiction?" she asked.

"You must remember, my deah," answered Dan, trying to speak in a Southern twang, "I *am* one of them."

"Right, I forgot you are, since we drove down here with a Pennsylvania license plate on our car and you couldn't stop talking about the New York Mets." She turned on the water to the shower.

"True story, but now that I'm back in my element of origin, 'this man in the South will rise again.'"

Mary Jo stepped into the bathroom.

Dan stopped the door as she tried to close it. "Would you like some help with putting soap on the places that are hard to reach?"

"That's quite all right. I can manage just fine," she said. "Besides, a real Southern gentleman would respect a lady's privacy. It's called chivalry, and you should know that." She gave Dan that sexy look as she unzipped her jeans. "The Southern man will have to wait until later to rise again."

∞

Friday night at The Watering Hole, pickup trucks filled most of the parking lot spaces. Dan hooked Mary Jo's hand as they walked to the entrance door. He did his best not to get too excited about her golden blond hair curling along the sides of her face. He tried not to leer at her yellow tee and her hip-hugging black jeans. He smiled to himself, knowing she was going to show these down-homers what a Yankee woman brings to the table.

As soon as they stepped inside, Dan could feel all eyes upon them. The patrons weren't discreet about it, either. Chatter all but ceased. They stared and they glared. It felt as if he and his wife had walked uninvited into their private home.

As Mary Jo pulled back his arm, he could sense her tension. The welcome sign was not out. "Maybe we should try some other place," she whispered in Dan's ear.

"There is no other place," he whispered back.

They found two vacant bar stools. When Dan pulled one back, a white-haired man with a face that had been weathered by too many days in the sun clutched his arm.

"This seat's taken," he said with a whistle through his teeth. "Charley's in the pisser. The one next is taken too. That's Billy Dixson's stool. He was Charley's best friend. Billy died six months ago, but we keep it open for him. He was one of the regulars here, so it's outa respect."

"Sorry," said Dan. He took Mary Jo's hand again, and they walked around to the far corner of the bar. Two seats near the exit door were open.

"These okay?" Dan asked the man behind the bar. The bartender slapped down two napkins without answering the question.

"I'll have a vodka tonic," said Mary Jo.

"Gimme a shot of Jim Beam and a bottle of MGD," said Dan.

"Going a bit heavy tonight, don't you think?" she said, trying not to make it obvious that she was counting the number of faces still looking their way. "I guess that makes me the designated driver."

"Just warming up for all the friends we're going to make in here," he whispered.

Dan scanned the perimeter of the bar. Most of the denizens had finally gone back to sipping their drinks and sharing small talk. Except for one.

"See the guy across the bar with the handlebar moustache, sitting with the woman whose low-cut dress leaves little to the imagination?" Dan asked.

"You mean the one whose boobs are pancaked on the bar?"

"Yup. Her manly friend there hasn't stopped glaring at us since we walked in."

Handlebar slugged down a shot of something, took a quick refill, and drained that one too. He wiped his mouth with the back of his hand and staggered out the door.

"Well, we know he's not leaving," said Mary Jo. "The bartender filled his glass again, and Betty Boobs is pretending she's not looking at us."

"He's in the parking lot. I bet he's checking out our license plate."

"Let's not jump to conclusions, Dan. Take another shot and relax."

He leaned back and glanced over at the far corner of the room where a band had set up drums, a guitar, and a keyboard. Dan figured they would be starting their gig in about fifteen minutes, at the nine o'clock hour. He watched someone drop a coin into a jukebox, expecting to hear Willy Nelson or Lynyrd Skynyrd. Out of the box came an old Garth Brooks ballad. Onto the dance floor stepped about ten couples.

Dan threw back two more shots. Handlebar had returned to his seat. He was filling Betty Boob's ear with something while never taking his eyes off Dan and Mary Jo.

The song ended. The dance floor emptied. After another shot of JB, Dan lifted himself off the barstool. Before Mary Jo could ask where he was going, he ambled over to the jukebox. Through the alcohol glaze in his eyes, he spotted a song that took his mind back to when he'd first twirled Mary Jo on a dance floor, where everyone had circled around them at the Playpen

Lounge in South Brunswick, New Jersey. He popped in two quarters and watched the 45 rpm flip over onto the turntable.

"Crimson and Clover" by Tommy James and the Shondells sounded its first unmistakable word. Dan spun around to look over at Mary Jo, who was already shaking her head. She smiled the same smile he remembered from that moment frozen in his mind. Swinging her legs around her stool, she pushed herself onto the floor. With a soft glow from the barroom lights behind her hips, she sauntered toward Dan.

> Ah when she come walking over
> Now I've been waitin' to show her
> Crimson and clover
> Over and over

Their eyes met. Their bodies came together. Hand in hand, Dan twirled Mary Jo around in a perfect circle.

They danced to that same rhythm, locked deep inside that other moment, once lost in time, now found in this place, in this town. Dan remembered to forget everything else so he could feel nothing but this special interlude with his beautiful lady.

The song faded, and they strolled hand in hand back to the bar. He heard applause coming from near the band stage.

"Very nice, you two," said a young brunette who was getting ready to sing with her band.

When Dan smiled back at her, another voice shouted from across the bar. "I reckon I'm gonna hafta disagree with you about that, Chrissy Lee. I don't like no Yankee ass stinkin' up our dance floor."

Mary Jo pulled Dan's arm. She led him around to the back of the bar where Handlebar was sitting. Just as he spun around on his stool, she reached onto the bar and tilted his glass of beer, spilling it over the back of his black sleeveless tee shirt. Betty Boobs screamed and jumped up nearly falling off her stool.

"You son of a bitch," Handlebar said slow and low.

"Not quite right, redneck," Mary Jo yelled back. "I'm not a *son* of a bitch. I'm the daughter of a Yankee bitch!"

Handlebar tried to rise from his stool. Dan figured he had only a second to act. He swung his right fist high and hard, catching Handlebar's jaw, knocking him to the floor. Betty Boobs tried to get off her stool, but Mary Jo pushed her back down. Dan had no time to admire his punch. His hand hurt like hell. Handlebar tried to pick himself off the floor. Wiping the back of his hand across his moustache, he grunted like a wild pig and jumped up to his feet. Dan swung again, but this time he missed. With his nostrils snorting, Handlebar charged. He drove his shoulder into Dan's chest. They crashed to the floor, knocking over an empty barstool on the way down.

"Git 'im, Digger!" somebody yelled.

While wrapped together in a bear hug, pain speared through Dan's back. He summoned up an adrenalin kick and rolled Handlebar over. He tried to grab the man's throat, but with a loud groan, his foe lifted Dan up and threw him to the side. Breathing heavily, Handlebar staggered to his feet while Dan tried to feel if the numbness in his legs would allow him to get up.

"C'mon, you Yankee bastard!" Handlebar raised his fists.

"Still fighting the war, huh?" Dan said from the floor through his gasps of air. "Were you at Gettysburg? Pickett's Charge?"

"My great-great-uncle was killed there by you Yankee bastards. Died right there on yer piss-putrid dirt. I reckon he cain't fight the cause no mo' but I sure cain!"

Handlebar rushed toward Dan but was stopped in his tracks by a clenched hand on the back of his shirt. The bartender stepped in front of Dan, who had finally picked himself up from the floor. "This little spat is over," said Chrissy Lee with her fingers still wrapped around Handlebar's collar.

"Both of you, shove your testosterone back down your pants and get on your damn stools!" she demanded.

Like scolded children, Handlebar and Dan returned to their ladies. A few chuckles of laughter filtered through the smell of stale beer and spilled whiskey.

Chrissy Lee, in her tight blue jeans and a low-cut, red-checkered shirt, stood behind the microphone in front of the band.

"Now, I don't care if you call it the Civil War or the War of Northern Aggression, but the truth be told it was American boys killin' American boys, and hell, that weren't right," she said into the mike. "So I'm gonna sing you two boys a song, a song sung best by the great Jennifer Nettles and her Sugarland band. It's just right for what I'm talkin' about. Put cause aside and jump into the shoes of a scared young boy walkin' across a field with a gun across his shoulder and his mom or his sweetie in his heart. He's starin' at death long before he could live his own life."

Chrissy Lee's words commanded a silence in the bar. Mary Jo swung her arm around Dan. He glanced over at Handlebar; Betty Boobs had rested her head upon his shoulder. "Here goes. One, two, three." She began to sing "Shine the Light."

Dan swallowed another bourbon, this one, long and hard. Mary Jo, misty-eyed already from Chrissy Lee's first verse, rubbed her hand lightly over the back of his shoulder.

The song, with help from the whiskey, transported Dan in his time machine. He was the Rebel boy again, facing the fear of death brought on by the war.

∞

Joshua marched across the battlefield with a new purpose, a different determination, not to kill but to find safe haven. Guns fired. Cannons blasted. Soldiers, wounded and bloodied, fell to the ground.

He kept going through it all, invincible and unharmed. Near the top of the hill, he came face-to-face with Death. A strange calm swirled around him, as if God had wrapped him in a blanket to protect him from the Prince of Darkness. Death stood right in front of Joshua, calling him forward with its bony finger.

"Get out of my way!" Joshua snarled. "Becky's waiting at the top of the hill. Becky! I knew you'd be there, Becky! I'm comin' home!"

Death laughed and took a step forward. Joshua threw a punch right into its black face. With a loud groan, Death crumbled into a swirl of dust and vanished with the wind.

∞

Chrissy Lee's words from the song jumped into Dan's head.

And when your worries, they won't let you
sleep and rob you of your days
And you've looked in all directions, but you
still can't find your way
Or when you just need someone to remind
you it's gonna be okay
I will shine the light.

Applause rocked the barroom. Emotion gushed from Chrissy Lee's eyes as she bowed before the patrons.

Handlebar shoved another shot down his throat. He left for the exit door, leaving Betty Boobs inside a frozen frown. Dan slid off his stool to head for the door. Mary Jo grabbed his shirtsleeve.

"Trust me," he said. "No fight this time."

As he walked by Betty Boobs, she stared him down. He threw her a thumbs up.

Out the door and into the chirps of the night's crickets and tree frogs, Dan approached Handlebar, who was standing next to a black pickup truck, smoking a cigarette.

"I'm Dan Bryant." He extended his hand.

"That right." Handlebar stuck the cigarette in his mouth.

"I've lived my whole natural life up North, but I have roots down here," said Dan, blinking his eyes through circles of the smoke. "That war, whatever we choose to call it, and, in particular, one Confederate soldier named Joshua Park brought me down here to find out some answers to questions I've been asking myself for a long time." Dan inhaled the white, humid air. "Joshua died at Gettysburg during Pickett's Charge. His body was never recovered. No headstone. Nothing but a memory that lives in my head every day. I'm here with my wife to find a descendant of a girl he once loved. She was from somewhere around here."

Dan lowered his eyebrows at Handlebar, who hadn't changed his manner one bit. "I just wanted to apologize for what happened in there, but I need to tell you that you don't really know me. And if you lost some kin in that war, well, I'm on your side about that, too."

Handlebar flicked away his cigarette. He looked up at storm clouds clustering in the twilight. "Digger Carter, that'd be me," he said. "Lost three kin in the war. One, my great-great-uncle at Gettysburg. His body were dug up from the field and brung back here. Now he's up in the hill there, next to two other that died on Rebel soil.

"I don't reckon you know what yer talkin' 'bout with that boy," Digger said. "I might think yer drunk or full a shit or both, but somethin' tells me you believe yer own story. So fer what it's worth, good luck tryin' to find his girlfriend's kin."

Digger lit another cigarette. "We still got some families down here who cain trace back to the war. Lost young boys and old men to the Yankee bullet. Hell, just up the road a piece lives Blanche Jordan. Billy Jordan were only thirteen when he were killed at Antietam. Then there's Molly Blackburn 'bout three mile up the road. Jimmy Blackburn were seventy-eight years old when he died at Shiloh."

"You said your last name was Carter. Do you know anything more about the man with that name who died at Gettysburg?" Dan asked.

"Stories say he were one mean sumbitch. Believed in family first, and he were a Southern man through thick and thin. I reckon he hated everyone from the North, and that included Lincoln. One story claimed he volunteered to Jeff Davis hisself to go an kill Lincoln right in the goddamn White House. Woulda saved a lot more lives if they woulda let him cuz he woulda got it done."

"All kidding aside, Digger, I know exactly who you're talking about."

Digger took a long drag from his cigarette and then coughed up the smoke. "You got a name for that boy's sweetie?" he asked.

"Becky," said Dan. "Rebecca, I guess. That's all I have."

"That name's about as common round here as a bullfrog in a pond."

"Well, I plan on going to the town hall tomorrow to find as many Rebeccas as I can that lived here in the 1860s."

Digger flicked his cigarette butt into the parking lot. "Lemme buy you a drink," he said. "It's how we make amends for disagreements round here."

Dan smiled. "You got any special bourbon in there?"

"Freddie keeps some forty-year-old bottles in the back. He'll pour us a couple a jiggers if I ask him nice."

Four jiggers later, Mary Jo was helping Dan to the door. A storm had rolled in. Flashes of lightning lit up the night sky, followed by loud cracks of thunder. Dan covered his ears. The rain pelted the parking lot like the rat-tat-tat of a jackhammer.

Mary Jo was frightened when she got behind the wheel of the rental car, a Ford Escort. Dan had just one clear thought from his booze buzz, making him wish he hadn't drunk so much. "Relax," he said to her, trying to keep the slur out of his voice. "Just take it nice and easy, and we'll be fine."

The downpour hammered the windshield so hard that Mary Jo had to flip up the car's wiper speed to warp five. No streetlights were anywhere as the road snaked along. Whenever a car came by, its headlamps flashed quarter-sized water droplets on the windshield, blinding all vision ahead. Dan would call this kind of storm a "white knuckler," and sure enough, Mary Jo's grip on the steering wheel had squeezed all color from her fingers.

"Nice and easy," Dan said again. "I'll watch the right side of the road. You watch the middle."

Mary Jo forced an uneasy laugh. "If I'd known this weather was coming, I would have been the one getting drunk so you could drive back to the hotel."

"By the way, I loved that mean streak that came out of you in the bar," he said. "Hell, the only thing that would have made the fight more fun was if you had dragged Betty Boobs by her hair out into the parking lot."

Just then, as Mary Jo maneuvered the car around a sharp bend, the high-beam headlights of a truck coming the other way blinded the windshield at the exact time loud thunder cracked

the sky. She screamed and whipped the steering wheel sharp-
ly to the right. As the car spun out of control and bounded for
the woods, she tried to turn the wheel back. The force from the
speed was too much. Into the woods they bounced through un-
derbrush and over fallen timber. Mary Jo screamed again. Dan's
body shot upward. He hit his head hard against the roof of the car.
Mary Jo screamed a third time. With all his might, Dan slammed
his body into her, pushing her body against the door. He grabbed
the wheel and slung his leg over to where his foot could reach the
brake. Just ahead, a cluster of trees stood in their path. Thinking
he couldn't swerve to miss them, he jammed on the brake pedal,
jerking both of them toward the windshield.

The car rolled to a stop inches from the trees. Their bodies,
recoiled just before their heads would have smashed through the
glass. Dan shifted the transmission into park.

"Oh my God." Tears filled Mary Jo's eyes. She leaned over
and collapsed on his shoulder.

"I told you we'd be fine," he said, trying to comfort her. He
peered through the wipers swinging across the windshield. The
rain had lessened a bit. A clap of thunder sounded in the distance, an indication the storm was moving away. The engine was
still running. "Honey, I gotta get out to see if we can get the car
out of here or if we'll have to call for help."

Funny thing, he thought. *Nearly getting killed in a car crash is
a great way to sober up after a night of hard drinking.*

He flung open the door and stepped out into a drizzle of
warm rain that felt like bathwater against his face. He couldn't
see any immediate damage. When he turned around to signal
Mary Jo, a man wearing a baseball cap jumped out of the dark in
front of him.

"Whoa!" Dan hollered. "Mary Jo, lock the car!" Dan
clenched his fists, hoping this wouldn't be his second fight of the
night. "What the hell do you want?" he asked with no intent to
exchange greetings.

The man smiled, exposing one missing front tooth and the
other so black it should have been missing.

"Yee haw!" shouted a voice from a long-haired man who was tapping on the driver's side window with the back of a flashlight. "Looks like we got ourselves a pretty li'l Yankee bitch sittin' in the car, jus' awaitin' for some real Southern men to come along and give her a good time."

Dan took a step back to brace himself against the car.

Black Tooth moved a step closer to him.

"Listen, we don't want trouble here. In fact, we could use some help to get back on the road."

"Oh, there'll be no trouble," said Black Tooth. "You wouldn't wanna bring no trouble with us, old man. That wouldn't be in yer best interests."

Long Hair tapped harder on the window. "Come outa there now, little honey. Show us what you got under that shirt and inside them jeans."

"Fuck off!" Mary Jo yelled through the window

"What'd ya say, Fern? Should I bust the window?"

"Mary Jo!" shouted Dan. "He raps that window one more time, put the car in reverse, and back up as fast as you can. Then run over the son-of-a-bitch."

Black Tooth pulled a switchblade from his pocket and pointed it inches from Dan's throat.

Long Hair reared his arm back to smash open the window.

Mary Jo tried to jerk the car backward, but it lurched forward.

Long Hair smacked the flashlight into the car window, shattering pieces of glass everywhere. "Get out, bitch!" he shouted.

Mary Jo flung open the door and jumped out. Long Hair slammed his body against hers, driving his knee into her groin. "Now, Yankee bitch, you can either take it nice and easy, or we can do it rough and tough."

"Let's do it rough and tough, asshole!" she snapped.

He drove his knee harder into her groin, lifting her body up against the car door. Mary Jo winced. She swung her right arm and raked her nails across the left side of his face, leaving three parallel red lines that oozed blood from his ear to his mouth.

Dan drove his fist into Black Tooth's belly, jackknifing his body in half. Another uppercut punch caught the reeling man's chin point blank, knocking him backward until he fell to the ground.

While Long Hair wiped the blood from his face, Mary Jo kicked him square in the crotch. He stumbled backward, grabbing himself, moaning. Meanwhile, Black Tooth pulled himself off the ground and thrust his knife at Dan, who backed up and stumbled over a log. Dan couldn't maintain his balance, and down he fell. Black Tooth raised the knife over his head. Dan attempted to roll over, but a searing pain ripped across his chest.

A gunshot blasted through the woods, and a bullet ripped into the back of Black Tooth's knee. The knife flailed from his hand before he collapsed to the ground.

"You hold on right there!" The voice came from behind a double-barrel shotgun that shifted from side to side. "Nobody moves just yet." The man came forward until Dan could see his stubbled face by the taillights of the car. "That you, Fern and Will? Thought so. Get over here, Will, and get on the ground next to your brother." Will shuffled over, still holding his crotch.

The gunman wore a silver sheriff's department badge. He took a cell phone from his pocket and tapped in a few numbers.

"Here's the deal," he said. "Will, you get your ass home right now while I call your old man. I know what Pap will do to the both of you will be worse than that buckshot I put in your brother's leg and the assault charges I'm gonna write up on both of you two tomorrow mornin'. Now move!"

Long Hair slumped his shoulders and walked slowly toward the road.

Black Tooth lay on the ground holding his leg. The lawman bent down. "Just a flesh wound, you candy-ass. Might lay you up for a week or so before you and that idiot brother of yours do some jail time." He stood back up, then reached down, grabbed Black Tooth's arm, and lifted the wounded man to his feet. "Now you limp on outa here before I shoot the second barrel of my shotgun right through yer other leg!"

The lawman turned to face Dan, who was leaning on the hood of the car to steady his breathing.

"Jack Dannin. They call me Deputy Jack around here," he said. "Sorry about this lack of hospitality. We really do have a lot of nice people in this town. Saw the Pennsy license plate. You on vacation?"

"Just in case anyone cares, I *am* still alive." Mary Jo came around the car to Dan, and they embraced.

Jack took a step back and allowed them to have a moment.

"If you hadn't come along when you did, there'd be a whole different story to tell about what happened here," Dan said.

"Thank you," added Mary Jo.

All of a sudden, Dan grabbed his chest and winced.

"Are you okay?" asked Jack and Mary Jo at the same time.

Dan took a deep breath. "I'll be fine. I must have pulled a muscle."

"Now how might that be?" Mary Jo snipped. "You're sixty years old, and tonight you had a fist fight with a bar hound, and then you had to defend yourself from a knife attack by a crazed sub-human being. You have chest pains after all that? Go figure."

"Well, if it comforts you to know this, I'll file a report tomorrow against Fern and Will Gathers for assault, but their biggest problem really *is* going to be with their old man," said Jack. "If I know Pap, they won't see the outside of their house anytime soon, and he'll ask the judge to throw the book at 'em, too"

Dan could offer no response to Jack. His mind fought back thoughts of rape and murder. All he could do was extend his hand, which Jack grabbed with a strong shake.

"Let me help you get your car out of here. I'll write an account of what happened for the rental car company. If you have a minute, I can meet you two for a cup of coffee at Smokey Joe's. It's just up the road apiece. It just might help calm you down from all this excitement.

The coffee was hot and strong, and Dan's night of drinking seemed as if it had happened days ago. Mary Jo looked exhausted—*as well she should*, thought Dan. A jolt of guilt punched him in his gut. He'd put her through so much. He would never question her love for him again. Dan reached for her hand and gave it a squeeze, feeling nothing in return.

Just for a second, he wished they were on a Caribbean beach drinking piña coladas.

"So, you never got a chance to answer my question back there. You on vacation, or do you have business in Lineville?" Jack asked.

"We're here on a sort of business," said Dan. "We're looking for a relative of a girl who moved to Clay County back in the early 1860s, someone who might still be living here."

"That's a long time ago. You got a name for this girl?"

"Becky or Rebecca."

"Last name?"

"Willow or Talley is all we could come up with."

"Well, I reckon that's not much to go on if you're gonna go to the municipal center to look up records," said Jack. "But just on a hunch, there was a Rebecca Willow who lived about three miles up the road before the war started."

As if on cue, Dan and Mary Jo leaned across the table. "Can you tell us more?" Dan asked.

"A little old lady named Anna May Winston lives in a farmhouse near there with her two cats. Her husband, Peter, died, oh say, a dozen years ago. Well, anyway, Anna May, she's in her nineties now, likes to talk about her great-grandmother, whose name was Rebecca Willow. Willow was her maiden name. Rebecca married a fellow, name I don't remember, but she married and had a daughter, who had a daughter, who had a daughter, and that's Anna May." Jack sipped his coffee. "I reckon that's about all I can tell you if you think it might help."

Dan leaned across the table.

"This Anna May," said Mary Jo. "Does she still have her . . . ?"

"Oh, she still has all her marbles," said Jack. "She does have one peculiarity, though.

"What's that?" asked Dan.

"She watches *Wheel of Fortune* every night and every day and every time I stop in to check up on her. She must have a thousand of the damn shows taped, and she watches them over and over again." Jack laughed. "I hear there's a campaign around town to raise money to get Pat Sajak and Vanna White to show up at her door one day."

Dan and Mary Jo laughed. "Could you do us a favor and ask her if we could come for a little visit tomorrow?" Dan asked.

"I could," said Jack, sipping his coffee, "but to be fair to Anna May, I think she would need some more information about what you want to know about Rebecca."

So Dan told his story, from the baseball game fireworks through the hypnotherapist to the vivid details about the life of Joshua Park and how Joshua became Dan Bryant. Mary Jo kicked in some incidentals that Dan had left out along the way.

"I know you may think I'm crazy," Dan concluded, "and I don't blame you if you do because I've thought that about myself so many times through all this."

Jack threw him a stare. "That's some story, but I believe you—why else would you have come all the way down here and almost get yourselves killed to find out about this Rebecca? You might very well be crazy, but if you're crazy enough to follow your belief this far, I think you should meet Anna May." Jack leaned over the table. "My curiosity tells me to ask you one more question."

"What's that?" asked Dan.

"What are you hoping to find out from Anna May or, better yet, from what she can tell you about Rebecca Willow?"

Dan looked Jack straight in the eyes. "I want to know why the hell a nineteen-year-old Confederate soldier would be reborn, if I can use that word, inside the mind of me, a sixty-year-old man who's never lived a day of his life south of New Jersey. Mary Jo and I are here to find out what we can about Joshua and Becky. And I'm pretty certain there's nobody left on Joshua's side for us to tell us anything." Dan finished his coffee. "Anna May might know something about the letter he wrote to Becky or, excuse me, that same letter I had in my hand when I died at Gettysburg." Dan realized how stupid all that sounded, how unconvincing, too. He half-expected Jack to jump up out of his seat and bolt for the door.

"Interesting. Very interesting," said Jack. "I mean this whole death-becomes-life-again business. Sometimes I think we can all come back to new life, but other times I think that when we die from this life, we all will see each other on the other side again, if you know what I mean."

"Yes, see you on the other side," Dan said with a sense he was speaking to an old soul.

"I'll tell you something else, Deputy Jack. I don't believe for one damn minute that you just happened to come along and rescue us from those rednecks."

"What exactly are you getting at, Mr. Bryant?"

Dan leaned back in his chair.

Mary Jo threw him a puzzled look.

"Never mind," said Dan. "Let's just call it my intuition."

"Well then," said Jack, "I guess I was lucky to have come along, and I hope you and the missus find your Rebecca."

"Thank you for the coffee, and again, thank you for everything else too," said Mary Jo. "Until you came along, I was thinking there wasn't a single kind person living in this county, other than a young woman who sang us a beautiful song at the bar earlier tonight."

"Chrissy Lee is just great, isn't she?" said Jack as he picked up the check. "She's the best show in the county. Well, it's time for me to get my report back to the sheriff. He's getting up near retirement age, and he counts on me to do a lot of what his arthritis won't let him do no more."

"If I get the chance to meet the sheriff, I'll tell him that you're the best man to take over when he retires," said Dan.

"Well, that would be a first for me. I might have been second-best at some things and the worst for sure at a lot of others, but I ain't never been the best at anything."

Dan pushed his elbow into Mary Jo's arm.

∞

On the ride back to the motel, Mary Jo poked Dan in his side.

"What was that hit with your elbow all about?"

"The wedding, Mary Jo," answered Dan. "The wedding that Joshua and Becky never had. Jack's name was Jenkins back then. He was going to be their best man. He was killed at Gettysburg, too." He took his eyes off the road and glanced at her. "Joshua and Jenkins never got the chance to meet again on the other side of that hill at Gettysburg." Dan peered over the steering wheel into the black of the night. "But they did meet again on the other side of their lifetimes."

August 12 – 3 a.m.

Sometime in the middle of the night, Dan awakened to find Mary Jo sitting up, crying. "What's the matter?" He pulled her head gently to his shoulder.

She chased back more tears to speak. "I just had a nightmare. Those two rednecks in the woods. This time I wasn't able to fight him off, and I guess I'm not as tough as you think I am."

"You woke up, honey. You woke up," Dan repeated. "I can hold you until you fall back to sleep."

"There's another thing that's bothering me. It's selfish to think of this right now," she said reaching for a tissue from the bedside table.

"What is it?"

"You may find out tomorrow the answer to a question that's been haunting you for too long now."

Dan was confused. "But isn't that what we've been looking for here, so we can get on with our lives?"

"Of course, Dan. But you can't see this whole thing through my eyes."

"What do you mean?"

Mary Jo's frustration was obvious. "You *are* Joshua Park."

"And?" Dan interrupted.

"And I am *not* Becky Willow or whatever her last name was."

Dan lowered his eyes. He had no reply to what she'd just said, but the implication of her words alarmed him.

"So," Mary Jo took a deep breath, "if there's any point to this . . . this chasing a ghost of a soldier, it would be that Joshua Park is wanting to hook up again with a reincarnated Becky somebody, so they can complete what they started a century and a half ago."

She makes so much sense, thought Dan. *All of it makes too much sense.*

Mary Jo put the tissue to her nose.

"So what the hell is my role in all this?" she asked. "Am I just supposed to be the other woman?"

"No, no, no. Don't think that way." That was all Dan could say. He could have told her she *was* the Becky reborn, but she would know he was lying.

"What if this Anna May tells you she knows a woman who believes she's Becky?" Mary Jo sobbed. "So what do you do? You go and find her. Then what? You shake hands, say it's nice to meet you, and just walk away?"

Dan needed to interrupt her chain of thought. "Yes, that's what I do. I walk away. I would think that we could put our past lives where they belong, in the past, and go on living the lives we have now," he said. "I just want to *know.*"

"That would be pointless," said Mary Jo. "That would mean that this dead kid's wish to renew his relationship with his girl-friend after all these years would simply end with a handshake. How satisfying is that? I mean, he came to life again through you just so you could find Becky again. You have to complete their love story."

Right again, thought Dan.

"First of all," said Dan, trying to think before he spoke, "there's no guarantee that this Anna May will lead us anywhere, especially to another woman in this universe who happens to believe she's a reincarnated Becky."

"It *has* to go that far," interrupted Mary Jo. "God, the stars in the universe, whatever or whomever you believe has put this boy inside your soul, wants you to find her. It's not just fate, Dan. It's *spiritual.*"

"Okay," said Dan. "So let's play it out this way. I have to find out why Joshua became me to find Becky. So be it. The three of us will have to figure out why all this has happened." Dan paused. He handed Mary Jo another tissue. "What if this Becky

Willow is a twenty-year-old woman or even a twelve-year-old girl?" he asked.

Mary Jo blurted out a laugh. "You've already proven you like your women young. Maybe that's it. Never thought that I, a woman twenty years younger than my husband, might lose him to someone twenty years younger than me!"

"What if she's a hundred years old?" Dan asked. "My point is that none of that matters. Do you think this Becky is sitting somewhere in a dark room waiting for Joshua to show up? What matters is, even if we do find each other, we don't throw away the lives we have in front of us."

Mary Jo put her head back on Dan's shoulder. "You make it sound so simple," she whispered. "I want you to find the answer, however that happens. We need to get on with our lives, raise our kids, and put the past behind us where it belongs."

"Let's see what tomorrow brings," he said. "Any way you look at this, we'll come to a finish line. If Anna May is our breakthrough or if she gives us nothing, then we go back home with just that."

"I'm praying she knows something," said Mary Jo. "Otherwise, all we take home from this trip are nightmares of rednecks and rotten teeth."

Jack called Dan early in the morning to have them meet him at Anna May's house at ten thirty. Mary Jo was primping her hair in the bathroom. "You'd think you're going to meet the pope the way you're fussing with yourself," he snipped and immediately ducked out of the way of a hairbrush fastball that smacked the wall behind him.

"Listen," she said. "If we're going to poke around inside the mind of a ninety-year-old woman, we'd better look proper and act proper so we don't frighten her into a heart attack. Besides, she might be related to one of those rednecks we encountered last night."

Just before they left the hotel room, Mary Jo made Dan go back and change his shirt. "Bright yellow makes you look like a used car salesman," she told him.

∞

Jack greeted them in front of Anna May's farmhouse. "I told her something about why you're here," he said. "She's fine with it all, but I'm asking you to keep your visit short. She naps after lunch, and then it's *Wheel of Fortune* marathon time. Now, I got to get back to take care of some business with the Gathers boys. You two take care, and have a safe trip back. I hope you find what you're looking for."

"We can't thank you enough for everything, Jack." Dan extended his hand. "If we do find Rebecca's new soul somewhere, maybe she and I will have a mock wedding, and we'll be sure to send you an invitation."

What a stupid thing to say, thought Dan, especially seeing the anguish on Mary Jo's face after he said it.

Jack tipped his cap before he drove off in his police car.

August 13 – 10:45 a.m.

The farmhouse stood high upon a hill like a grand monument of Southern history, representing a proud heritage of Alabaman architecture.

Dan and Mary Jo ascended the porch steps. He noticed a white wooden rocker on the porch. The chair must be where Anna May sat on warm summer days, rocking and looking out to the countryside, reflecting on her ninety-some years of life experiences. Like a vehicle driven over a hundred thousand miles, the chair had little tread left on its wooden tires.

He imagined that, once inside, they would be greeted first by a musty smell of old age from the walls and furniture. They'd enter a room that looked unlived-in, except for one chair with faded upholstery and crocheted doilies on its back and arms.

Dan reached his index finger for the doorbell. He felt as if he was about to press a button that could open a library filled with stories of his past life. His heart raced, and his face flushed. He took a deep breath and pressed. The bell elicited a familiar Westminster ring-tone.

The door opened a crack. Behind it a tiny, white-haired woman in a white housedress dotted everywhere with red roses appeared. She looked up at him from the back of narrow glasses. Her lips formed a slight smile. "You must be Mr. and Mrs. Bryant. I have been expecting you," she said with a crackle in her voice. "Please come in."

They followed her into a living room. Two cats scowled at them and then scooted toward the back of the house. Dan had guessed right. The furniture looked new for being old, except for a blue wing-back chair adorned with three white doilies. No musty odor permeated the air, though. A scented candle on a small round table lifted a tinge of lavender into the room.

The old lady motioned with her hands for them to sit on a couch that was across from her chair. "I'm Anna May," she said. "When I said I've been expecting you, I meant that I've been expecting you for quite some time. When Jack told me you were coming, I said to myself, 'My Lord, how about that. The day has finally come.'"

Dan shifted his eyes from Anna May to Mary Jo, who dropped her jaw at the comment.

"Thank you for allowing us to come into your lovely home," said Mary Jo.

"Yes, we really do appreciate your willingness to accept a visit from total strangers, especially ones who have travelled all the way from Pennsylvania," Dan added.

"Well, sir," she said with a laugh, "please pardon my disagreement, but one of you two is not a total stranger." Anna May took a breath and spoke again. "I know why you're here, Mr. Bryant. I've been waiting for you for a long time. I just didn't know who you would be or where you would come from."

"How—I mean, excuse me, Ms. Anna, but what do you mean you've been waiting for me?" Dan asked.

"Well, I believe now is the time to let the cat out of the bag . . . , Parky," the old woman said with another laugh. "You *are* Joshua Park, are you not? Or at least you were, a lifetime ago."

Dan's heart skipped. Mary Jo reached for his hand. Until hearing this kind old woman's startling words, his belief in his past identity had never been more authenticated.

"Joshua Park," Dan repeated.

"Yes, sir," replied Anna May.

"Becky Willow?" Mary Jo asked.

"Yes, ma'am," she replied again. "Rebecca Jean Willow, daughter of William and Lucille Willow, is my great-grandmother."

She had announced Becky in the present tense, as if the calendar had flipped back to a day in 1863.

"The Willows lived across from a large wheat field just a few steps from here," Anna May continued. "Their house is gone now. My house was built on family-owned land in 1914. William, who was Rebecca's father, died in a horseback accident when she was two years old. Rebecca lived with her mother.

After the War between the States ended, Rebecca was courted by a young Confederate colonel named Charles Andrews. They married and lived across town. She had one daughter, Beatrice, who grew up to marry a wealthy railroad man from the North. Beatrice had a daughter named Eve, and later on, of course, Eve had a daughter named Anna May. I believe you now know who she is.

"Excuse me a moment, please," Anna May said. "I think you might enjoy a cup of tea." She stood up, anchored her legs into a steady position, and then shuffled out of the room.

"Can you believe we got this lucky?" Mary Jo asked in a whisper.

Dan leaned forward from the couch. He dropped his head into his hands, trying to maintain his sensibility about everything that had led up to this moment, this house, and this woman who was proving to be the missing link between Joshua, himself, and Becky.

Anna May returned with a silver tray and three rose-pattern teacups that nearly matched the flowers on her dress. "Milk or sugar?" she asked.

"Thank you," said Dan and Mary Jo together.

She returned to her chair where she let herself down gently. "Mr. Bryant, before Rebecca died, she made sure that Beatrice knew all about Joshua and that Beatrice would pass it all down to me." Anna May sipped her tea. "You see, she married this Charles Andrews, who tried to capture her fancy with flowers and high-style fashion and the finest treasures that money can buy, but Charles never captured her heart. I do not believe he ever related to her spiritually, if you know what I mean. To you, sir, who now clearly holds the soul of young Joshua Park—Rebecca's heart has always belonged to you."

Mary Jo squirmed on the couch as Dan exhaled and took a sip of tea. "Well," said Dan, "Becky, or as you call her, Rebecca, hasn't given me a clue as to where I might find her in her new existence."

"In the Lord's time, she will find you, and you will have no doubt that she will have Rebecca's soul."

"Ms. Anna May, was all this knowledge about Becky and Joshua passed through Beatrice to you by word of mouth?" asked Mary Jo.

"Not entirely. As a very little girl, I did spend a brief time with Rebecca, and of course, I have been told much about her. She was someone who you might say was quite different from a gentile Southern lady. She spoke like a barroom Jack and laughed like one too. She had her gentle and loving sides, and as I said before, my family was amazed at her sense of wonder. They used to say that Rebecca might have had her feet on the ground, but her head was always in the clouds.

"Now to answer your question, you might recall a letter she wrote to you . . . pardon the awkwardness, Mr. Bryant, but my mind wants to know you as Joshua for the moment."

"That's just fine," said Dan. "I died at Gettysburg with her letter in my hand, but for whatever reason, I have no recollection of its contents. It was lost forever with my body."

"No, sir," said Anna May. "Rebecca wrote a copy of the letter because she feared you would not return. Then Beatrice made a copy, and I have made a copy as well. And now I can pass the letter along to you."

"Oh my God," said Mary Jo. "You have this letter here?"

"Yes, ma'am. I also have the original letter that Joshua wrote to Rebecca."

Dan looked at Mary Jo. "Can you believe this is happening?"

"It's so amazing to me, Anna May, that you knew this day was coming," said Mary Jo.

"Oh, there was never any doubt that I would live to see this day. When you read the words in their letter, you'll understand that our meeting each other was guided by Rebecca's faith in the spirits. When she and Joshua asked for a second chance to be together, the good Lord was certainly listening and taking notes."

Dan glanced over at Mary Jo. He could tell she was disappointed again that she wasn't a major character written into this astonishing story.

Anna May continued her tale. "You see, Rebecca had a good life with Charles Andrews, rest assured of that, but she had given away her heart to you, Joshua, and that's where it remained for all her years on this Earth. Even when she was just days from death, her eyes would widen like a child's whenever she would speak of her afternoons with Parky."

A perfect silence filled the room after Anna May's remark. Dan was anxious to read the letters but tried to hold his excitement back. This remarkable lady seemed to sense his impatience. "If you both could follow me into the back room," she said, rising again in her careful way.

Once there, she led Dan and Mary Jo to a glass case. She tapped on the top with her finger. Dan saw a piece of paper, yellowed with age, torn at the corners, with another tear through the center. He could barely make out the faded handwriting at the top.

"My Dearest Becky," he read. "April 23, 1863."

"When Rebecca determined you had died, she ripped it. She threw the letter into a drawer, where it remained for years and years. Finally, she passed it along to Beatrice, who had someone preserve it in this glass case."

She lifted her hand and placed it on top of Dan's trembling fingers.

"When you find Rebecca, she is to be given this case," she said. "You must take it with you today, as I have no one of such importance to leave it to."

Anna May walked over to a drawer, where she lifted out two more pieces of paper. "Here are legible copies of their letters. One is your letter, and the other, Rebecca's letter to you." She handed them to Dan. His fingers fumbled to open them, but Anna May grabbed his hands. "Not here," she said. "You must read them where they were written," she said with a reassuring smile.

"Where?" Dan asked with a pitch in his voice.

"Ol' Oakie," she said. "You and your wife go and walk the back field until you reach their big oak tree. That's where Rebecca and you, at different times, wrote these letters."

"I know so much about them, and I know about these letters too—but if I'm Joshua now, why don't I remember what I wrote?"

"Joshua has given you his soul. What comes with that is a window to his physical life. Spirits of souls keep secrets until proper times and the proper places come together for them to be revealed."

She paused and placed her hand against Mary Jo's forearm. "The spirits move with the wind across the sacred field by Ol' Oakie. My family has always believed this special place is a sanctuary for souls."

Mary Jo reached over and hugged Anna May. "You are an extraordinary woman," she said to her

"No. No," said Anna May. "I'm just a keeper of hearts. The extraordinary lies within your husband's soul and in the one you have yet to find." She took both of Mary Jo's hands in hers. "And you, young lady, do not despair. You too are playing an important role in this love story."

Dan took Mary Jo's hand as they stood at the edge of the field. The expectation of what would appear at the end of their journey through the reeds was almost too much for him to bear. To slow the rapid beating of his heart, he decided to summon up a song.

"Sing with me," he said to Mary Jo.

"Sing? Sing what? Johnny comes marching home again, hoorah?"

Dan laughed. Mary Jo laughed. He broke into song, a favorite tune of his long before he could imagine that the words would fit this scene just as the glass slipper fit Cinderella's foot.

> Will you stay with me, will you be my love
> Among the fields of barley

Mary Jo picked up the cue. They sang the lyrics with an energy that seemed to lift their footsteps above the narrow path to the tree.

> I never made promises lightly
> And there have been some that I've broken
> But I swear in the days still left
> We'll walk in fields of gold

The tops of the reeds reached out to touch them both as they walked hand in hand through the field. Anna May had told them they needed no map of direction. The spirits would guide their journey to Ol' Oakie.

"There!" Dan pointed front and center. "There it is."

Appearing in the distance like a fabled king behind his city of gold, the great Southern live oak towered above the horizon.

"Spectacular," whispered Mary Jo.

They walked faster now. From twenty yards away, Dan noticed a clearing off to the left where the field changed its complexion.

"Look for the sacred circle," Anna May had said to them when they were departing her house. "When you enter the circle, you will know this is your very special place."

Dan could see it now—a ring of blue and yellow wild flowers that surrounded the tree of life.

Just ten more yards to go now. Ol' Oakie's massive trunk must be thirty feet in circumference, thought Dan, *and nearly a thousand years old.*

Once into the sacred circle and under the tree, they cast their eyes up and into this extraordinary creature of nature. The oak reached sixty feet or so into the early afternoon sky. Dan wondered what had happened here during the passing of so many years that this icon of history had witnessed. If Ol' Oakie could speak, it might tell the stories of the once living, of the forever loving, and of those who have returned to drift above the wavering field.

The oak's bark, textured by centuries of seasons, felt to Dan's imagination like the skin of an immortal and wise old man. "Ol' Oakie," he said aloud. He placed his arms around the trunk as far as he could. He looked up through its limbs again, some lifeless and leafless, that shadowed and cooled the ground from the hot sun with an umbrella of hanging moss. And then he began to remember what Joshua had known.

His mind's eye saw Becky sitting on one of those giant limbs, swinging her legs back and forth into the fresh air.

"It's beautiful," said Mary Jo. "I mean everything here is just beautiful."

Dan turned with his back to the trunk and faced the field. An adrenalin rush shivered his body. Standing under this tree behind this field that the spirits had preordained as the setting for a reunion of lifetimes, Dan relinquished himself to Joshua's soul. He sat down on the ground and drew his knees up to his chin. He aligned his senses in harmony with the serenity of this sacred moment.

"Mary Jo," he said, "take out the letters."

He reached out his hand, but she pushed it away. "Let me read Becky's to you first," she said. "I can get a feel for her voice."

My God, he thought. *What a woman!* All their issues and conflicts, their age difference, none of that mattered anymore. Rebecca Willow had come into his soul, but Mary Jo belonged in his heart.

She carefully opened Becky's letter, removing a large leaf from between the fold.

"Anna May places a new leaf inside the letter every year," said Mary Jo. "When you started to walk to the field, she called me back to tell me that Becky and Joshua believed that their love would be kept safely within the strength of this tree until they could be together again.

"Are you ready?" she asked.

He nodded.

A gentle breeze swept across the field. Dan felt its cool touch upon his face. Mary Jo's hair lifted from her forehead.

> Dear Parky,
>
> This letter will be all you will have of me until you come home again.
>
> I cannot truly speak my fears in words, but my heart misses a beat each time I think I may have to live my life without you. Since the day I saw you sitting under Ol Oakie, I knew you were different, yet different like me. Our minds thought about wonders that were invisible to the eye. Our souls were driven by the energy of this field that lay before us. We felt something together that no one could have ever imagined would be possible.

As you face the dangers of war day after day, I pray my spirit can bring you peace of mind and, of course, keep you safe from harm so we can be together again.

There is so much more I wish now that I would have said before you left, but I lacked the courage to do so.

I love you, my sweet Parky, and I have faith that the spirits of our field will help you return. So for now, I will feel you close to me each time I hug Ol' Oakie. I will listen for your voice whenever the wind sweeps across our very special place.

If we cannot have this life together, I will wait a thousand years until we can have another.

Loving you forever,
Becky

"Read the last line again," Dan said, staring into the sway of the reeds.

"'If we cannot have this life together, I will wait a thousand years until we can have another.'"

Dan inhaled a breath of the fresh air. "It's time I read my letter to Becky."

Mary Jo removed the oak leaf from inside the flap before passing the paper along to Dan. She folded Becky's letter and put the leaf back inside. As Dan began to read, a new breeze wisped through the field toward them.

My Dearest Becky,

With our promise kept, you are reading this letter because of the obvious reason.

I would think you to be taken aback and sad for a time, yet I hope to God that your grief be not long.

The sun will rise again tomorrow. Live your life, my sweet love. Never lose your extraordinary spirit that happened upon me that afternoon we met under Ol' Oakie.

I have a new promise that will cast a new light on our love.

Upon our last days together, we spoke at length about the spirits in the wind that sweep across our golden field. We observed a beautiful orange butterfly dance from flower to flower, merely touching one bloom and then others before lifting its wings to a particular yellow blossom where it rested, until with new energy, it flew high above the field.

I place my trust in our love we have for each other, that like the butterfly has now been lifted into a long flight above the clouds.

Dan felt the lump in his throat grow larger until he could no longer speak. He handed the letter to Mary Jo.

The brutality of the battlefield cannot kill what lies within our souls.

Death is not final. It cannot destroy my will to be with you again.

My faith was a gift given to me in these words from my mother and from Joseph Charles.

Keep faith in what I believe is true.

My dear sweet Becky, I will always believe in us.

Like the butterfly searching for the perfect flower, my spirit will fly in the wind until it finds the perfect soul that will have a new life with you.

Understand that nothing in this life can be returned to its original exactness. Leaves that fall from Ol' Oakie will die, but new life will soon sprout again. The new leaves will be unlike any leaves that have lived before. Our rebirth will bring two new hearts together in a different and exciting love.

This is my promise.

I have begun my journey to return to you into another time when a new soul born from my essence will find your new soul born from your spirit.

Then once again we will dance upon our field of gold.

Forever yours,
Parky

Dan rested his back against Ol' Oakie. His mind relieved itself of everything, other than the perfect silence rising above the field, kissed by an approving sun.

A welcomed quiet commanded the drive back to Jim Thorpe. When Dan and Mary Jo did speak, they talked about seeing the kids and pushing the button to restart their normal lives.

As he turned onto the interstate, Dan came to an affirming realization. He didn't care as much anymore if he found the new Becky Willow. If she was out there somewhere, then let her find him. He had discovered his own truth under Ol' Oakie, and the final event of this journey had removed all his anxiety, leaving him with a peace of mind he had never felt before.

When they arrived home, he placed the glass box with the letters inside a cabinet in the basement where they would be preserved within a constant cool temperature. He had no interest in reading them again anytime soon.

Late August

The kids went back to school. Katy was now a fifth grader, while Jacob entered the tenth grade. She took piano lessons, and he played fall baseball.

Mary Jo increased clientele for her holistic nutrition business. Dan coached Jacob's fall ball team. As he expected, the outcomes of the contests were building character in his son.

In one game, Jacob had three hits and pitched a no-hitter, but the very next day, he failed twice to come through with the game on the line. He had climbed to the mountaintop and crashed and burned into the valley below, all within a twenty-four-hour period.

Jacob experienced how baseball parallels life. Good days. Bad days. You win some, and as Dan had preached, you never lose; you learn.

Although Jacob showed signs of getting what his father meant, Mary Jo would remind Dan that the boy was too young to have the confidence and courage to pick himself back up so soon up after he got knocked down. That's when Mom stepped in to wrap her arms around him and say everything was going to be all right. After another game in which he didn't play well, she made Jacob his favorite dinner of chicken parmesan with mashed potatoes to let him know there was still goodness left in his world.

October 5 – 2 p.m.

On an unusually hot and humid autumn afternoon, Dan pitched batting practice. Preparing his Lazars for their big game against the Crush, he stood behind the L-screen and fired ball after ball to his young hitters.

"Contact with the ball is not the end of your swing," he told Jason. "Get your bat around until your chin sits on your front shoulder."

"Swing only at strikes," he said to Jarod.

"Pivot off your back foot," he corrected Casey. "Get your belly button to the ball. That means your hips rotate properly."

Sweat dripped from Dan's forehead. His shirt was glued to his chest. He wiped his brow with the back of his pitching hand and looked down toward Corey. The kid seemed a bit out of focus. Dan tried to blink away the blur when a sudden charge of pain enflamed the inside of his head.

Corey stood ready to swing. Dan blinked again and again. A burst of intense heat raged through his chest. He thought it might be the sausage he had eaten at breakfast.

"You ready, Stevey?" he called.

"Coach, I'm not Stevey. I'm Corey."

"Oh. Right. Sorry, son."

Dan pulled back his arm. Pain seared across both shoulders. When he let go of the ball, he was already in free fall. He tried to reach out his hand to break his downward crash, but it was too late. Dan hit the ground face first.

"Coach!" he heard somebody yell.

"Dad! What happened?" Jacob shouted.

A dull, thick pain throbbed inside his chest, running down his left arm. He gasped for air.

"Oh my God!" were the last words he heard someone scream before his eyes shut off the light of the afternoon sky.

October 5 – 4 p.m.

Dan opened his eyes. "What just happened? Where the hell am I?"

He turned his head to see Mary Jo sitting next to his bed. "What . . . ?"

"You're in the hospital, Dan," said Mary Jo. "You had a heart attack. The doctor will be bringing in further information soon." She kissed him on his cheek. "This isn't the way you want to go out. Instead of playing baseball with the kids on your team, you're supposed to have the big one while you play batter-up with me." She wiped a tear from her eye.

The doctor entered the room. He was a large man with graying hair. "Mr. Bryant, I'm Doctor Browning. I'm glad to see you're resting comfortably. You lost consciousness on the baseball field, and you were lucky that one of your players' mothers is a registered nurse. She administered CPR to restart your heart."

Dan couldn't process everything he'd just heard, but the doctor kept talking.

"Our tests show that you have a condition called ventricular fibrillation." He raised his eyes and looked straight at Dan.

Mary Jo reached out to take his hand.

"It's a disorder of your heart's rhythm. We're going to pre-scribe an anti-arrhythmic medication to try to stabilize your heartbeat."

"I guess this means no more skydiving or running marathons?" Dan said, trying to keep the calm in his voice.

"You'll need rest, and keep activities to a minimum until we see if the medication takes effect."

"No baseball?"

"No baseball unless it's with your eyes only. Not until we see you in a few weeks. Let me give it to you as straight as I can, Mr. Bryant: Your heart stopped beating on that field today. If it weren't for that nurse, it's unlikely we would be having this discussion. And you don't have to go anywhere to thank her. She's right here."

In walked Tyler Banner's mother. She smiled as she came toward Dan. With Mary Jo's assistance, Dan struggled to sit up.

"Saying thank you just isn't enough." Dan opened his arms.

She reached over the bed for his embrace. "Believe it or not, your heart started up pretty quickly," she said. "The real challenge was calming down the parents and the kids."

"What about Jacob?" Dan asked.

"He's okay now. He's out in the hall waiting to see you," she said. "I think he was in shock. He didn't cry until we got him to the hospital and he saw his mom."

It was as if all sound ceased to enter Dan's ears. He lay back down in his bed for an "oh my God" moment. What had just happened was life altering on so many levels that he tried without success to shove back the improbabilities from his mind. *Mary Jo would have been left a widow to raise Jacob and Katy. Can I ever throw a baseball again? Play catch in the backyard with Jacob? Dance in the living room with Katy? Make love with Mary Jo? What now? Do I just lie down and wait to die?* He closed his eyes to squeeze away his fears.

"I love you."

Dan opened his eyes when he heard Mary Jo's voice. He looked up at her, thinking he might already be in heaven when, just for a second, he thought he saw wings upon her shoulders.

"You've slept a lot, and that's a good thing," she said. "I brought Jacob a half-hour ago just to show him you were resting comfortably. He left with my dad. Mom has Katy. All is good at home."

Dan frowned. "As much as we didn't want to face this, the moment has finally come."

"What are you talking about?" she asked.

"You married an older man who is now a dying old man."

"You want me to go get a shovel now? I can dig you a hole somewhere right outside the hospital's main entrance."

"Let's be serious, Mary Jo. We've pretended this day would never come. When you said yes to this older body, you wrote yourself a script to become a widow long before you should be."

"Don't you think I realized that? Before we marched down the aisle, I went through all the scenarios of living life without you. Then, when I had the cancer scare, I thought, *So, this is what God was planning. I go first, leaving you with the kids.* Now that you have this attack, it's just the way it's supposed to be, Dan. There's no getting upset. We face this as we've faced every other damn thing that has gotten between us."

Her face filled with anger. "How dare you insult me, Daniel Bryant! If you want me to feel sorry for myself for marrying a man who might die tomorrow, then you must think I'm some kind of idiot who will be too pissed off to bend over your casket to give you a final kiss."

"Well," said Dan, "that's certainly a heartwarming thought. By the way, when you lean over, I hope you're wearing that Michael Kors perfume just in case I have some sense of smell left."

"You have become exactly what you don't like about me." Mary Jo leaned over to lower her voice. "A sarcastic pain in the ass!"

"You always have the right words to say to make me feel better," he said. "Please don't ever get soft on me, Mary Jo. Keep the insults coming!

Their lives were on the clock now. Life together would tick away by the days, the hours, and then the final minutes. The end, though uncertain as to the when, would be the number of his heartbeats until the laws of subtraction counted them down to single digits. He would never look at time on a clock again.

March 1 – 2 p.m.

Months passed. Seasons changed. Dan built a dollhouse for Katy in the basement. He cooked gourmet recipes during February snowfalls, some thumbs-up, some thumbs-down. Once in a while, he trashed his health watch to down a few Bacardi and Cokes to numb his mind from his nagging heart telling him to always be careful.

Mary Jo flitted about the house, pretending life was normal. She made an obvious effort not to become Dan's caretaker. He helped her clean the house. Together they took care of the children's needs. There was no talk about health or dying, except when they visited his doctor to get the "all okay" sign or, as Dan had put it, the safety squeeze sign rather than the suicide bunt.

Lovemaking became seldom and guarded. This was when Dan felt the worst about himself. He told Mary Jo that she was free to have an affair with a younger man in the prime of his life.

She said she was attracted to a guy at the gym with bulging biceps. "You're lucky," she joked. "He came up to me the other day and wanted my advice about asking another man he just met for a date."

The kids were being kids, going to school, laughing, playing, and at times aggravating both of their parents until they heard the "stop or else" command.

As the weather warmed, the major leagues announced pitchers, and catchers were reporting to spring training, Dan spotted an ad in the local *Times-News*.

Get a hit off Iron Mike. Win bicycles for the whole family, valued at $500. All you have to do is

bat a ball fair against the state-of-the-art, comput-
erized Iron Mike pitching machine that throws
98 miles per hour to different areas of the strike
zone. Five dollars for one pitch only. All pro-
ceeds go to the local community baseball league.
Guaranteed strike-zone pitches. Bunting and half
swings are allowed. Any contact that stops a ball
in fair territory wins the bicycles. Come to the in-
door complex at the Hitters Edge in Whitehall on
Saturday morning, 9-10 a.m.

After reading the ad to the family at breakfast on Friday,
Dan announced, "Let's go!"

Jacob laughed. Katy twirled her spoon in her cereal. Mary
Jo frowned.

"You really think Jacob can get a hit off that thing?" she asked.

"No, I think he's a bit overmatched swinging at a ball that's
coming in at one hundred miles an hour."

"So, if he can't hit it, why go?"

"Because *I* can."

"You can what?"

"I can hit the ball."

⌒∾⌒

A line of men, women, and children stood outside the
entrance door of the Hitter's Edge. Dan figured the baseball
league was going to make a couple hundred dollars in the
scheduled hour.

Iron Mike loaded up and began firing baseballs to men,
women, and children of all ages. No one even came close to putting the ball down into the fair territory, marked off by a strip of
turf in front of home plate. Bunters failed. Big swingers looked
foolish. Some were so overpowered by the speed of the pitch they
never even took the bat off their shoulders. One middle-aged
man managed a foul tip that brought a roar from the crowd that
continued to grow.

Mary Jo remarked to Dan that he should be wearing a dunce cap rather than a batting helmet.

Dan studied the machine, watching its grip on the ball and its release point.

"Watch this next pitch," he said to Jacob. The ball fired into the inside lower part of the strike zone, winning another five-dollar contribution. As another hopeful stepped into the batter's box, Dan said, "This pitch should go to the outside corner."

Jacob watched the ball drill the lower outside of the strike zone net.

"How did you know that?'

"It all depends on how the ball falls into the flipper arm of the machine," explained Dan. "If the seams form an upside down U, the ball will go inside low. An upright U, it will be outside corner. A U that faces left will be a middle high strike. That's what it will throw now. A U facing right will be up and in."

The next batter swung and missed at a middle high strike.

"Wow, Dad. That's amazing."

"I will have exactly two seconds to recognize the grip before it pitches to me," said Dan with an air of confidence.

"But you still have to hit the ball," said Mary Jo.

"Not hit it. The ball just needs to hit the bat and land fair. If I try to bunt, the ball still has a good chance of going foul."

Dan examined the next grip of the machine before it fired away.

"The ball has to hit a surface that is about the same diameter."

Dan took his place in line. No one since the man who had managed the foul tip had made any contact with the baseball.

Finally, Dan got his turn. He stepped into the box, holding a thin-barrel metal bat on his right shoulder. He stared out at Iron Mike as if the machine were a real pitcher staring back at him. The ball fell into the loaded position, and the flipper arm started to move forward.

Just before the arm snapped the pitch, Dan pointed his bat like a rifle toward the machine. In the quarter of a second, the 100-mph fastball reached the hitting zone. Dan held his bat steady.

Plunk.

The ball bounced straight down in front of home plate. It rolled six inches forward until it came to a stop in fair territory.

A wake of applause broke out around the batting cages. When Dan walked out, people mouthed the words, "How did you do that?"

∞

"When the weather warms, let's take our new bikes for a ride along the old gravity railroad tracks down to the Lehigh River," Dan said on the ride home after he had whistled a few lines from Creedence's "Lookin' out My Back Door."

"You said you could do it, and you did, Dad!" said Jacob from the back seat.

"I had a little help," Dan said.

"Did you cheat somehow?" asked Mary Jo. "Who helped you?"

"Cheat? Well, if I did, no one will ever be able to tell."

"You did have very good hand-eye coordination when you played baseball," she said.

"True, but I needed more than just me today."

"So who helped you, Dad?"

"That boy who could line up his rifle barrel and shoot off an enemy's fingernail at thirty yards away."

"Joshua's bullets were outgoing," Mary Jo smirked. "That fastball was incoming."

"It worked both ways with him and with me," said Dan. "When I was nineteen, I could throw a ball through the hole of a donut in one try."

"Really, Dad," said Jacob. "A baseball doesn't fit through a donut hole."

"You're right, son," Dan said. "But a golf ball does."

October 14 – 3:30 p.m.

Dan pitched Wiffle balls in the late afternoon sun to Katy. On his third throw, she smacked one high into the windy sky. The ball sailed into Jessie's backyard where it came to rest beneath the big willow tree.

"Daddy, I'm cold. I want to go back in the house."

"Okay, honey."

Dan walked across the yard to retrieve the ball. He saw Jessie sitting under the tree, her back resting against its trunk. She held a large maple leaf, colored by autumn's yellow crayon. A sudden gust of wind lifted the leaf from her hand; it floated upward and then took a sharp turn into the direction of the drifting clouds, flying high over Dan's head toward the back of his yard.

He followed the swirl, keeping it in his sight. Another gust of wind lifted more leaves into the flight.

Dan stepped under the vortex until the breeze subsided and the leaves floated to the ground. He took his eyes off the pile to see Mary Jo standing erect in the yard, holding a single yellow maple leaf in her hand.

"Whatcha got?" Dan asked in a child's voice. "A special yellow one?"

She handed him the leaf. His eyes opened wide. A heart had been drawn inside its raised veins with an inscription penned into the center.

BW + JP

Dan pointed the leaf at Mary Jo, who hadn't moved an inch.

"Becky Willow and Joshua Park," she said. Dan could tell Mary Jo was holding back something else she wanted to say.

"Becky?" Dan asked in obvious confusion.

Suddenly, he heard rapid breathing behind him. Turning around, he saw Jessie standing there, appearing exhausted from her run across the yards. With her face painted in fear, she looked at Dan but only for a second.

Dan's mind blinded her from his sight. A different image jumped into his vision, a face etched into his memory from a long time ago. "Becky?" he asked. "Becky!" he said again, this time with a volume of conviction.

Jessie reached out her hand, and Dan placed the leaf upon her palm. She tried to run away, but Dan grabbed her wrist.

"No! No!" Jessie shouted. She turned her back.

He didn't let go of her arm. "It's okay, Jessie. You don't have to be afraid."

"No!" she cried through a rush of tears. Dan loosened his grip on her arm.

Jessie turned around, and this time she fixed her eyes upon his. "Josh-u-a?" she asked. "You can't be. I don't want you to be!"

"But I am," said Dan within a breath of emotion. "And you are Becky. It's how I said it would be in my letter to you. We would have a new life together."

Jessie cocked her head like a confused puppy, just as Becky had.

"You're not to be with me this time," he said.

The fear had lifted away from her face. Dan took the leaf from her hand.

"You see this leaf?" he explained. "It looks like all the rest that came from the tree, but if you compare it to the others, it's different. Nothing that once was can be original again. Joshua and Becky had their time. They asked the spirits above the field to grant them another chance, and now they can be together again."

Jessie opened her mouth to speak, but she paused as if she was summoning words from her memory. "Our love may have been shared just a few days in our time," she said with her eyes closed. "It will drift in the wind until a new soul, born from your essence, finds my new soul born from my spirit."

"Jacob," Dan whispered, as he looked down at the leaf in her hand.

He fell to his knees and felt Jessie's fingers upon his shoulder. From the ground, he gazed up at her, knowing she could now love his son with not one but with two souls.

Jessie helped Dan stand up, pulling him into her arms. While they held each other, he could feel himself as Joshua holding Becky.

Jessie rested her cheek upon Dan's pounding heart.

Then, just as Becky had run from his sight so many times through the field, Jessie broke free and sprinted across their yards until she disappeared behind the trunk of the willow tree.

With a gasp of relief, Dan shifted his eyes to Mary Jo. She stood smiling with her hands together as if in prayer.

"The willow tree . . . Becky Willow," she said. Why didn't we know?"

Mary Jo reached her arms around him, and Dan now knew she understood her own significance in this beautiful love story.

October 15 – 9 a.m.

The morning sun threw a beacon of light to guide Dan's steps as he walked the path to the overlook. The autumn air heightened his awareness of the woods. Stepping over a fallen tree, Dan reached his arms up to grab at a low-lying cloud. He laughed at a crow as it flew by and squawked its discontent toward him.

Dan and Mary Jo had made a pact with Jessie to not speak to Jacob about the revelation of the leaf. Dan remembered his promise to tell his son the complete story about Joshua and Becky, but as a father, he believed now that Jessie should choose the appropriate time and place to tell Jacob everything, with his father and mother present, of course.

But on this very day, Dan felt his ailing heart jump with joy. He reached the overlook, a three-hundred-mile vista of mountains and valleys divided by the Lehigh River that twisted along the old switchback railroad. He climbed upon a large rock where a Native American must have looked out upon the splendor of Mother Nature. This was the perfect place for Dan to ponder the perfection of his own existence.

He sat down on the rock and looked over the valley below and then to the sky above. An exhilarating thought entered his mind, and he giggled aloud like the child he had never been.

Life is everlasting.

October 15 – Noon

When Dan returned to the house, there stood Mary Jo in the kitchen holding the phone. "It's a Reverend Martin from Grace Baptist in Hazelton."

"Who's he?" asked Dan.

"No idea, but he sounds frantic."

He took the phone from her. "Hello?"

"Mr. Bryant? Reverend Martin from Grace Baptist Church. I have a crisis here in our backyard, and I think I could use your help."

Dan narrowed his eyes. "How does this involve me?"

"Toby Waterson is dressed in his Confederate uniform, and he has built a small fortress around himself behind our church. He's holding a rifle, Mr. Bryant, and this is certainly *not* one of his reenactments. When I tried to speak with him, he asked me to get out of his line of fire. He said he's going to shoot anyone who enters what he's calling his holy sanctuary."

There was a moment of uncomfortable silence on both ends of the phone line.

"Mr. Bryant, I'm terribly afraid that Toby will act upon his threats, and someone innocent will be harmed."

"Have you called the police?" asked Dan.

"Not yet. I'm trying not to alarm the neighborhood and to stop this before the media or the authorities get involved. Nobody, especially Toby, needs this kind of publicity. I remember him telling me about your connection with a Confederate soldier in the war, so I thought you might help. It's early in the afternoon, so I doubt any of his re-enactor friends are available. He left his cell phone in a church pew, saying he wouldn't need it anymore.

That's how I found your number. I'm pleading for your help, Mr. Bryant. Can you come here and try to reason with him?"

∞

As soon as Dan arrived, Reverend Martin greeted him in the church parking lot and led him around the front of the church to a small backyard. Dan saw a makeshift fence constructed from tree limbs and branches that Toby must have carried to the location. He spotted the top of a Confederate cap just above the fence line. A Confederate flag, hung from a tree branch, was posted in the ground.

"I tried to speak with him again," said Reverend Martin. "He says he has to protect the land of the Lord from the devil's bitch who wants to kill another Waterson and destroy his homeland. He told me again to get out of his line of fire or I might become a casualty of war."

"Did you tell him I was coming?" asked Dan.

"No. I was afraid that if he thought I was trying to stop him, he might do something irrational."

"Reverend Martin," Dan said, "I believe he's already done something irrational."

Dan looked across the yard again. Toby leaned over a pile of sandbags and raised his rifle.

"I'll talk to him," Dan said.

"Be very careful, Mr. Bryant. I have not told his wife about this. She's back in Alabama and with their infant son. Perhaps you can speak about his wife and their child, so he might realize what's at risk here."

"Toby!" Dan yelled from the edge of the grass. "It's Dan Bryant. Remember me? I'm one of the good guys."

"If you have come to join me to fight the devil's army, why are you not in uniform?" Toby shouted back.

Dan had to think of a quick answer. "I may indeed join you, but my present soul is urging me to talk about your intentions first." He thought about how stupid that must have sounded. "May I approach your abatis?" Dan wondered if Toby understood the word, pulled right out of a Civil War glossary.

"You may enter my abatis," he replied.

Toby's fortress, built with a circle of neatly stacked sandbags, surrounding a patch of grass, stored two bayoneted rifles. Dan spotted a coffee pot next to an open bag of beef jerky. A Bible lay on top of the sandbags in front. Three bottles of water were lined in a row next to the flag.

"It's not the camp I wanted to set up," said Toby. "I thought of putting up a small tent behind me, but since I'm behind enemy lines, I need a complete 360-degree view of their territory." Toby pointed to a plastic bag. "I have enough beef jerky and energy drinks to sustain me for a few days if need be." He propped himself upon his knees. "Good thing we have some modern conveniences."

Dan said nothing in return. He had to think of a plan to put common sense back into this confused young man's head.

"You must be thinking that I'm crazy," Toby said, motioning for Dan to kneel next to him. "When my granddaddy died at Gettysburg, he sacrificed his life to stop the imperialism of the United States government. They had no damn business coming to his homeland and telling him how to live his life." Toby spat onto the ground. "And the bastards are still doing it today. The White House continues to compromise our freedoms. We gotta make a stand. Start a revolution with a new civil war.

"I expect to go down in a blaze of glory today, just as Granddaddy did in the name of Jesus." He glanced at Dan. "You got the guts to join me, Joshua Park?"

"Who did you call me?" Dan asked.

Toby spat again. "You heard me just fine." He picked up his rifle and peered over the barrel toward the church parking lot.

Dan felt something inside him that seemed to arrive with a sudden gust of the wind. He looked across the lawn, but instead of the churchyard, he saw a battlefield blazing in the afternoon sun. He rubbed his eyes, not once but twice, until the field became the churchyard again.

"By the way," said Toby, handing an envelope to Dan, "if you come out of this skirmish unscathed, could you see to it that my missus and my son get this letter? If we both should meet our maker today, Reverend Martin will find a copy in the vestibule."

Dan shoved the envelope into his back pocket. "What if there are more bluebellies out there than we can kill?" he asked.

"You always were a bit timid, Joshua Park. Maybe the good Lord forgot to give you your testicles. I reckon it's time you grow a pair now."

"You might be right, but I reckon it's better to be scared than foolish, and by the way, since when does the good Lord want you to go out in a blaze of glory?"

"The Lord has enlisted the Waterson name to fight the devil since the very origin of our DNA. This is our family destiny."

"Do you want your son to grow up without a father as you and so many other Watersons did?" Dan asked.

Toby said nothing to the remark.

Joshua Park, and not Dan Bryant, reached out and picked up the other rifle. He could see a group of men mingling across the field. Then he saw men and women carrying large black objects with what looked like gun barrels protruding from their fronts. If they were weapons, he had never seen the like of them before.

With an effort to summon back his own will, Dan Bryant cleared Joshua's visions from his eyes and realized that the police and the media had arrived. Guns pointed at them from every angle. Cameras and boom mikes, threatening weapons in their own right, stood atop three television trucks.

Toby wiped something from his eye. "To answer your question, Joshua, I have prayed that my son will carry my legacy with him. Better he remember the relentless courage of his father than the cowardice from a man who surrendered to a tyrannical government led by Satan himself.

"The world you are talking about passed us a long time ago," Dan said, grabbing Toby's shoulder. "Better your son have a living father who can show him that the power of love can never be defeated by evil, rather than a disillusioned soldier whose paranoia becomes the cause of his death."

"Courage needs no gun to defeat this tyranny you speak of," said Joshua Park and Dan Bryant through one voice.

Someone called out. "Mr. Waterson! This is Channel Thirteen News. We would like to speak with you about what you're doing!"

Another voice sounded from behind the black line of cameras. "Toby! Mr. Bryant! This is Reverend Martin. I'm begging you in the name of the Lord to put down your guns and come out. Please, gentlemen. We don't want anyone to get hurt!"

Joshua, and not Dan, peered over his gun barrel. He saw flashing red lights from the road, what he thought were fireballs from incoming cannon shells.

"We are on hallowed ground, my friend," said Toby. "The ghosts of our comrades stand behind us. Thousands and thousands of our compatriots have come to be with us once again. In memory of their names, the South shall rise again!"

Dan's mind pleaded with Joshua to help him save Toby Waterson. "We take this stand on sacred ground behind this church of Jesus Christ," said Dan. His voice took on a chiding tone. "Tobias Waterson, your granddaddy spoke to me about the gift of life that God gives to every human being," said Joshua, willing his voice through Dan. "God wants *all* life to be protected and preserved." Becky's words now came to his lips. "No life should be lost to a pointless cause brought upon this country by the politics of misguided men."

Joshua's finger trembled as he placed it on the trigger of his rifle.

"Toby Waterson," said Dan, "in the name of the Confederate States of America, for the sake of your wife and your child, and to prove your granddaddy did *not* die without purpose, put down your rifle, pick up your Bible, and walk with me into this church to sit before the Lord and Savior."

Dan put down his gun.

With tears rolling down his face, Toby laid down his rifle. His trembling hand searched for the Bible. His fingers found the book on a sandbag. He stood up, and with both hands, he thrust the Bible above his head and faced the growing crowd that had flooded the churchyard.

A gunshot rang out.

A bullet punched a hole right between Toby's eyes. He spun around until he faced Dan. Toby opened his mouth, and with an involuntary convulsive movement, he dropped his hand and squeezed Dan's arm before he collapsed across a row of sandbags.

A sudden sweep of fresh air charged through the small fortress. Dan looked down at his hands, both covered in Toby's blood. He stood up, fully expecting to be shot in the chest again by another bluebelly—but this time, the bullet would come from a Hazleton police officer's gun.

"Step forward with your hands up," shouted a voice from behind a megaphone.

Dan relinquished his will to a command from his soul. He took Toby's Rebel cap from the ground and placed it upon his own head, pulling the brim down to rest just above his eyes. To honor the Rebel code, he would not raise his arms. There would be no surrender today. He pulled the Confederate flag out of the ground and grabbed Toby's Bible. He placed Toby's letter inside the front cover.

"Get your hands up and step forward," said the voice, flat and merciless. "Make no other movements, or you will be shot and killed."

Dan walked in Joshua's familiar steps carrying the flag in his right hand and Toby's Bible in his left. The guns from the blue-bellies were pointed at him from every direction.

"If you make any unnecessary movements, you will be shot and killed," repeated the voice.

Dan raised his chin. His legs, unsteady at first, found their balance, and he marched forward in movement with a familiar tat-tat-tat of a drum beating in his mind. He reached Reverend Martin, whose face was covered with tears.

Two policemen grabbed Dan. They tried to cuff his hands, but he pushed them away. A leather-faced man dressed in a blue suit jumped out in front and moved nose to nose with Dan.

"Your friend made a motion that was perceived by one of our officers to be an act of aggression, so we had to take him out."

Dan glared into the man's eyes and thought to say something. Instead, he thrust Toby's Bible into his face. The detective yanked it down, and Dan saw that same bullshit smile he remembered from the park administrator at Gettysburg.

"You will have to come with us, Mr. Bryant."

"My name is Joshua Park," Dan replied. "Private first class of the Alabama Thirteenth.

A sudden and heavy weight dropped into his chest. Dan stumbled to the side and fell into the outstretched arms of Reverend Martin.

October 15 – 6 p.m.

Following an intensive medical exam, tests revealed that Dan had not suffered another attack to his fragile heart. The detective from the Hazelton Police Department took the doctor's advice. Dan was sent home to rest and would be questioned at the end of the week.

On the drive home, every time Mary Jo braked the car, she nearly put them both through the windshield. Usually a harsh critic of her driving, Dan simply rocked back and forth with the hard stops and said nothing.

A half-mile from home, Mary Jo broke the silence.

"What the hell is his wife supposed to think? That her husband was crazy? He didn't give a shit about his baby? I mean, what the hell? At first, it was just a cute story about a kid trying to relive his love life, but now somebody's been killed, Dan! When is it all going to end?"

Mary Jo turned the car up their street.

It wasn't going to end just yet.

Cars and trucks lined both sides of the street. In the driveway, a crowd of people walked in circles and carried signs.

You killed Toby Waterson!

Reincarnation is the devil's lie.

Ask his widow and child if they care about your war story!

You're going to hell where all the rednecks belong!

"Oh my God!" said Mary Jo.

"Are the kids inside?" asked Dan.

"Yes, they're with my mother."

As they turned into the driveway, Dan could hear shouting from both sides of the car. One man slapped his hand on the window. "You murderer!"

The car lurched forward, nearly hitting an old woman who swung her sign across the windshield. Mary Jo maneuvered into the garage, pressing the remote to close the door behind them.

"I'm calling the police," she said to Dan as they entered the house.

"No need to," said her mother, who stood at the end of the hallway with her arms around Jacob, Jessie, and Katy. "They're already on their way. I called ten minutes ago."

In her usual quiet way, Mary Jo's mother told them the intruders had arrived in a parade of vehicles with their signs and their chants. She had gone to the door to ask who they were. One woman said they had come from Toby Waterson's church in the name of God. They wanted to confront the devil for stealing the soul of a good man, a pillar of the church, a family man who had never shown irrational behavior until he had met Dan Bryant from Jim Thorpe.

"I'll go out to speak to them," said Dan.

"Are you crazy?" cried Mary Jo. "Your heart can't take another strain like that! Don't you think you've had enough excitement for one day? Let the police come and get them all out of here!"

"Remember where you live," answered Dan. "This is a state police matter. They won't be here for at least another half-hour."

"So we sit and wait," argued Mary Jo.

"Jacob and I will come out with you," said Jessie.

Hand in hand with Jacob and Jessie, Dan walked out onto the porch. They were greeted with shouts and signs thrusting into the brisk evening air. Dan raised his hands to quell the crowd. He tried again.

"If Toby never met you, he'd be alive and with his wife and baby today," cried out a woman.

"You may be right about that," Dan shouted back. "Toby was a victim of circumstance, and I am a significant part of that circumstance. There was an angry force inside him. He wanted to avenge his grandfather's death." Dan rolled his eyes across the crowd. "Just before he was killed, Toby made the decision to live for his family, rather than to die for his cause.

A police officer killed him because he perceived the Bible in Toby's hands to be a weapon." Dan nodded. "The policeman was right. Toby's Bible is a weapon, and it should be used whenever love is threatened by evil.

I cannot explain to you what Toby and I have lived with inside our souls for such a long, long time," Dan said. "But with his final breath today, Toby left a message that has traveled within his soul for well over a hundred years: If we want to fight evil in the world, we must do it without guns, without violence. We fight with our love for family, and we fight with our faith in God."

Dan heard another voice in his head, not Joshua's this time, but that of Joseph Charles. "With faith, we believe in what is right, and then we must do what is right." Dan pointed his finger at his chest. "You can count me as the one who pulled the trigger today if you so choose, but now I am asking you to trust your faith and do what's right for Toby. Go back to your homes and pray for his soul. Pray his wife will understand Toby's sacrifice. Pray their son will carry his father's courage and grow up to be a peacemaker in this troubled world."

Two police cars pull up behind the crowd. Out stepped four officers. "Okay, everyone, we're asking you to leave peacefully and to vacate this man's property," announced the one in front.

The crowd dispersed.

A woman turned to face Dan. "What about you, Mr. Bryant? Why don't you carry the anger that Toby felt in his last hours?"

Dan sighed. "Ma'am, my calling was to restore love lost to lives that were ravished by war. When Toby looked at me today with his final breath already gone, his eyes told me that he died with that same love in his heart."

She nodded. "May God bless you, Mr. Bryant."

∞

When everyone had left the yard and the police had walked back down the driveway to their squad cars, Dan stepped back into the house with Jacob and Jessie. He kissed them and Katy and his mother-in-law on their cheeks, but when he got to Mary Jo, he kissed her lips.

Dan turned and walked up the stairs, leaving everyone and everything from the last 145 years behind him.

He entered the dark bedroom. Nightfall's moon appeared to be asking permission to come in through the window. He opened his hands and placed his palms on the cool glass, inviting the moonlight to slip between his fingers and soothe his tired eyes.

Eight Years After

Dan rose from the breakfast table. As he had done in thousands of yesterday mornings, he tiptoed to the sink where Mary Jo was washing the breakfast dishes and kissed her cheek. She returned her usual morning hug.

"I'm going shopping with Katy today," she said. "Do me a favor and throw in a load of wash. There's not much to do with just the two of us."

"You got it."

Mary Jo looked wistful. "It's funny, you know? I used to watch the kids grow through the changes in the sizes of their clothes. I complained about doing all their wash, but now that they've moved out, I actually miss washing and folding their laundry." She wiped a plate and glanced through the kitchen window at a chickadee that had landed upon the bird feeder.

"I can't tell you how many times I've looked out this window," she said. "And how about that willow tree next door. It's a living history book, don't you think?"

"Every tree tells a story," he said.

"Oh—Jacob said he might stop by to see you. He's dropping Jessie off next door. She and her mother are going shopping for baby clothes."

Dan kissed her again.

"What's with that?" she asked. "Did you take one of those little blue pills this morning against doctor's orders?"

"You just look extra beautiful this morning," he said.

"That reminds me. I need to make an appointment with your eye doctor. You need new glasses."

"I think I'll sit down and watch the news. I'm feeling a little tired at the moment."

"Katy's staying for dinner. She doesn't go back to college until Sunday. Maybe you can make chicken carbonara. You know that's her favorite."

Just then, the backdoor opened. "Hi, Dad," Katy cheered. She hurried over to give Dan a kiss.

"I just told Mom how beautiful she is today, and so are you, my little guppy."

"Dad, when you are you going to stop calling me guppy? I'm a big girl now."

"Never. As long as you give me your little-girl smile, you'll always be my guppy."

"We better get going, honey," Mary Jo said. "I want to start back before the work traffic hits Route 80."

"Bye, Dad. See you later."

"Let's have dinner around six," Mary Jo said as she followed Katy out the door.

A short time passed. The front door opened again.

"Dad, are you here?"

"I'm in the family room."

Jacob appeared, holding his father's baseball glove in his hand. He dropped a baseball inside the pocket and flipped the glove onto Dan's lap. "I offered to cut Jessie's parents' lawn. How about after I'm done, we have a catch?"

"Absolutely," said Dan.

"You know, Dad, you've stayed true to your word. You've always said yes to having a catch with me."

"You know I can still bring the heat," said Dan with a smile.

"I can't wait until our son gets old enough to throw a ball with you."

"Tell you a secret. Don't tell Mom I told you, and don't tell Jessie. We already bought the little guy a plastic bat and ball, along with a glove that his hand will have to grow into."

Jacob threw an approving grin back at his father. "I'll be right back. It'll take me only a few minutes to cut the grass."

After Jacob left, Dan put on his Mets cap and slipped the glove onto his left hand. He took out the baseball and punched the pocket twice. As he looked down into the worn leather, his mind traveled back to that time of long ago, back to his field of gold. He closed his eyes, and the scene became more vivid, as if he were watching a movie inside his head.

A young boy and girl are running through the reeds, chasing a shadow of a bird flying under the hot rays of the summer sun. Voices drift across the field.
"Parky, come catch me!"
"Where are you?"
"Right over here!"

He sees Jacob holding Jessie's hand in the shade of the back-yard willow tree. He hears them chatter in voices from that other time and from that other place.

Mary Jo appears, her eyes aglow.

Katy jumps up from behind her and whispers to him, "I love you more."

He sees his father, now young and virile, waving a baseball glove to come and play catch.

A sudden, heavy squeeze below his right shoulder takes Dan's breath away. Pain rips across his chest and shoots down his right arm, numbing his fingers. He squeezes the ball once and then drops it onto his lap where it sits for a second before rolling onto the floor.

He sees his mom with Dad and his two sisters, standing next to Joshua and Becky. They're waving to him. He moves his legs to run to them through the field, but an angel swoops down and lifts him into the sky. She reaches below him and wraps the field around his body in a blanket of liquid gold.

Higher and higher, they rise above the clouds until he hears a gentle voice welcoming him back home.

Eternity

Baseball players came straight from the field; one, a high school shortstop named Brandon, arrived in full uniform covered with dirt from head to toe.

Relatives and friends filled the church. Jacob and Jessie sat in the front row. Katy sat alongside her grandmother and Jessie's parents.

With the prayer service completed, Mary Jo stepped up to the podium. She lifted her chin and looked out upon the congregation. She cleared her throat, looked down at a piece of paper, and began to speak, knowing that her first words would command the attention of the room.

"Many years ago, I discovered my husband was in love with another woman."

A collective gasp filled the church.

"She was much older than I am, a century and a half older to tell you the truth. Her name was Becky, and she lived in Alabama where she was left with a promise of eternal love from a boy named Joshua Park, a Confederate soldier who would be killed in the American Civil War. Somehow and in some way, Dan was chosen to inherit Joshua's soul. And after that came a long journey until we discovered that Jessie, now Jacob's loving wife, has been gifted with Becky's spirit. To continue this incredible love story, Daniel Joshua Bryant will be born in a matter of weeks."

When Mary Jo looked down to find her place, the funeral director hurried up to the podium. He whispered something to her, and she nodded to him.

At the front door of the church stood four men displaced in time, dressed in Confederate army uniforms. Upon a command of "for'ard march," they approached the casket in perfect step. The soldier in front carried a large Confederate flag. The other three rested rifles upon their shoulders. As they neared the casket, an elderly man jumped up from a middle pew and stepped into the aisle.

Jacob stopped him.

"That flag is a disgrace! It's disrespectful to your father!" said the man.

"It's okay, Sam," said Jacob. "Dad would have wanted this. Go sit down, and you'll know why."

Sam gave Jacob a puzzled look before he returned to his seat. Mary Jo lifted her hands to quell the din in the room.

"Company halt!" shouted the lead soldier.

The four men formed a line across the front of the casket.

The man to the far left, sporting a gray beard down to his chest, removed a piece of paper from his pocket and began to read:

> Jesus, savior of this soul
> Let him to Thy bosom fly,
> While the waves of trouble roll,
> While the tempest still is high!
> Hide him, O Savior, hide,
> Till the storm of life be past;
> Safe into the haven guide,
> Oh, receive his soul at last!

> Other refuge has he none,
> Hangs his helpless soul on Thee;
> Leave, ah! leave him not alone,
> Still support and comfort him!
> All his trust on Thee is stayed,
> All his hope from Thee he brings;
> Cover his defenseless head
> With the shadow of Thy wing.

A young soldier from the far right placed a small Confederate flag upon the casket. In unison, the four men stepped back and saluted.

"Company, about face," said the soldier in the middle. "For'ard march."

Down the aisle they marched, oblivious to the glaring eyes of a confused congregation.

After the last soldier departed, Mary Jo again raised her hands to silence the chatter. "What you have just witnessed was a ceremony to honor Joshua Park of the Alabama Thirteenth Regiment. Joshua was killed at Gettysburg in 1863 and never received a final military tribute until today."

Mary Jo peered over the podium toward her family.

"To borrow an expression from a sweet old lady from Alabama, Dan and I were just the caretakers of hearts until we could set them free once again." Mary Jo wiped a tear from her eye. "And as long as love will never end," she said, "life can never end."

She stepped down from the podium and returned to her seat next to Katy. Jacob hugged her. Jessie kissed her and took Mary Jo's hand to rest upon Daniel Joshua.

∞

Upon leaving the church, Mary Jo saw a black man standing next to someone who looked like Deputy Jack. Together, they nodded to her at the doorway.

The congregation mingled under the light of the bright afternoon sky. A sudden breeze swept across the churchyard.

At that precise moment in time, from somewhere to everywhere, families of monarch butterflies danced across fields of gold.

THE END

Acknowledgments

I WRITE NEWSPAPER COLUMNS, sports stories, front-page features, and even a play here and there. You might think that with all these literary experiences, I would have conquered the words of this story without hitting too many bumps in the road. *Au contraire.* I hit all the bumps and a few potholes, too.

Truth is I was trying to maneuver the car with a broken steering wheel down a street so dark I couldn't see past the beginning or know where I was going to end. So with no map to follow, I threw caution to the wind, stepped on the gas, and lurched forward.

My wife, Stacie, went along for the ride, from the first uncertain word to the final punctuation mark. She listened, even when she was preoccupied. She shook her head at some ideas and nodded at others.

Following the sunrises of so many mornings, I read nearly every chapter aloud to her, and believe me, her critical suggestions were both necessary and appreciated. Otherwise, I would have slammed on the brakes and parked the car. What Stacie did not realize was that her spiritual energy drove both the evolution of character and the complexity of theme in this book.

Without her acceptance of my trembling hand in marriage twelve years ago, my story, in words borrowed from the poet Langston Hughes, "would be nothing more than a dream deferred."

My children, Richie and Sadie, provided the light of childhood in my eyes as I poured my love of baseball and young innocence onto these pages. Fatherhood is undoubtedly the best gift my wife has given me, and each time I look at my children being children in our house, I thank God for keeping me at their emotional age.

Selecting a friend to read through parts of the manuscript was risky business. Would this person provide honest criticism or undeserving praise? Early on, I tested the waters with my dear friend Terry Sawicki. Both she and her husband, George, have been with me through wonderful and worrisome events in my life, so I decided to trust my writer's fragile psyche with Terry, who is an avid reader of my newspaper columns. She raised my wavering level of confidence so I could keep on keeping on, especially during those predawn sleepless hours when the silent world outside my doors allowed me to summon the voice inside my soul to speak to the pages of this book.

Along my route down Robert Frost's road not taken—and by the way, it *has* made all the difference—a few critique partners helped me with my revisions. David Pollard, an emerging writer from Texas, Joanne Lesher, a member of my writers' group, and Karen Cimms, an author and newspaper co-worker, all deserve to have their names scroll down my list of credits. A special thanks to Joanne, who took the initiative of requesting my first draft after hearing me read just a few excerpts at our writers' group critique sessions.

I named my main character in gratitude to a man I have known for only four years. Dan Chimenti, a consummate risk taker and dream-doer, advised me to jump out of the airplane and build the wings on the way down. And now I can fly.

Finally, I must acknowledge my soulspeak.

The idea that I was listening to voices in my head urging me to write this book is not the truth, which hopefully eliminates the possibility of my name finding its way onto any list of the mentally unstable. No, the voices that pushed my fingers across the keys of a word processor spoke from deep within me, and although I hold no burden of this proof to my readers, of this I can be certain and ask you to accept: Joshua's voice helped me tell our tale, this extraordinary story that justifies our existence on so many levels. All I needed to do was believe in the power that lies inside the essence of my spirit.

Perhaps you too can begin an incredible journey that completes the circle of timeless love just by doing what I did.

Listen to the voice in your soul.